All of Me

Navajo Code Talkers Book 3

Eileen Charbonneau

Print ISBNs
Amazon Print 9780228637950
Ingram Spark 9780228637967
Barnes & Noble 9780228637974
BWL Print 9780228637981

Dedication

In memory of a would-be Code Talker,
Sophie Yazzie (1914-2019)
and for all the women who have served.

And to the memory of wonderful John
Wisdomkeeper (Métis),
who supported this series at BWL. I am
forever grateful, John.

"I don't stand up and say another culture is
no good.
We exchange ideas and knowledge and
look for the good in both...
That is a bridge."
--Carl Nelson Gorman (1907-1998) U.S.
Marine Corps Platoon 382,
first class of the Navajo Code Talkers

Table of Contents

Chapter 1

Summer, 1943
Riordan Railroad Station, Arizona

Reunion

Luke Kayenta checked the delicate gardenia nestled between two rapidly warming bottles of Pepsi Cola. Was it foolish to bring the corsage, given the train's tendency to be late in wartime? But it had called out to him. *I am for her, the one you left in those other canyons,* it had said.

He sensed Kitty Charante every day and deep in the night. He sensed her while waiting for mail deliveries. He caught the scent of her fingers, past all those fingers that had handled her letters between the city of New York and the small Dinètah trading post where they finally reached him. That scent she wore—Eau de Gardenia always intensified when they kissed.

His mother and sisters teased him about the corner of his sister Taswan's window where he nurtured the small plant that had flowered in time to welcome her. It was where he kept the small stack of books, photographs, and drawings from Kitty and her family. Even his grandmother, who did not tease him as much, called it his shrine. Did their laughter signal approval of the correspondence across their cultures?

His nephews accepted the gifts of baseball cards and marbles from Matty and Dom, their counterparts in Kitty's world. Maybe the children should have come here to the station to wait for her arrival with him. She was used to family all around her.

Where was the train? He stood, leaving the gardenia on the bench, and paced, a bad habit he'd picked up from White people.

A Hopi woman, who had been scowling at him since he'd shared the shade beside her, stirred. "She is coming," the woman said, in English, their common language.

Under his own shoes, Luke now caught the vibration she'd already felt. "You are right, Grandmother," he said in the best Hopi he could manage.

She grinned, her eyes disappearing in the squint. "Come, lovesick newcomer. Help these old bones to rise."

He obeyed, giving her his arm, grateful she had used one of the less pejorative terms her people had for his: newcomer. The Hopi had preceded the Diné into the American Southwest by many centuries.

As for the "lovesick," that was merely a statement of fact.

Kitty saw him from the window as the train slowed. Through the shimmering heat he stood in his full-dress uniform, with every button fastened, gleaming. His hat shaded his eyes. And a gardenia was somehow blooming in his hands.

"The war must be going badly if the Marines are letting them in," the conductor said, behind her. She turned. He shrugged. "Waiting for that gaggle, likely." He gestured to the laughing woman, who lifted a baby as her two small girls waved from the train car window. It was the family Kitty had invited to use her private compartment's washroom an hour earlier, to place a Band-Aid for the older girl's scrape. "Elbow's the strongest part of you if anybody gets fresh," she'd advised as she worked. "I know," the girl replied with a small smile.

"I don't see anyone waiting for you, Mrs. Charente," the conductor said now. "You'd best stay on. Flagstaff is a proper stop. You can telephone your party from there. Put it back, George," he instructed the stooped porter, whose name was not George.

The train lurched. The edge of her trunk bumped the smaller girl off her feet. The mother quickly transferred the baby to Kitty, then lifted the crying girl.

The conductor sighed hard. "Now, Ma'am, you don't have to help these clumsy—"

"Stand aside," Kitty ordered.

Even the crying girl went silent.

The porter, a small barrel-chested man, turned, grinned wide enough for her to see his gold tooth. "No lasting harm done? Well, this way then, ladies and children," he proclaimed brightly, hoisting the mother's carpetbag on top of Kitty's trunk.

The older sister blocked her way. Her pretty embroidered blouse was like her mother's. Unlike her mother's braid, the girl's black hair was whorled around each ear. "You can't keep our *tiposi*, White lady," she warned.

Her mother's breath caught.

Kitty laughed. "Don't worry, kiddo." She looked down at the still-sleeping infant. How long had it been since she'd allowed herself to hold a baby? *Breathe,* she told herself. *You can do this.*

The scowling girl came closer, tilted her head. "You don't smell like iodine now. You smell good."

"Thanks. How's the elbow?"

"Better." She pointed her chin out the train's last window. "Is he your man?"

"Sure is. Isn't he handsome?"

The girl frowned. "He is Diné. But my grandmother pets his arm. Look, *Ingu!* Grandmother pets a Diné!"

"Hush," her mother admonished, her younger child now settled at her hip. "My daughter is very young, Miss."

"I have five years," the girl protested. "My sister has three, but she can jump rope almost as good as I can." She nodded toward the bundle in Kitty's arms. "He cannot even sit up yet. But he likes to laugh."

"Well. You're all swell kids. Even him."

A smile broke through the woman's wary expression. "You honor my family."

As the train door opened, the heat hit Kitty with a force that rocked her stance. She was still getting used to the altitude change from New York's sea level. This was a new challenge. But the baby nestled in her arms balanced her. Careful. Baby's wiseacre sister was onto Kitty's deep longing. The piney smell of his head only intensified it.

Luke Kayenta reached out for her. She remembered his hands and their gentle strength. He eased her down the train's steps, traded the baby for his gardenia with a shy smile. He carried the baby back to his mother. The Pullman porter left her trunk on the platform and carried the young mother's bag to the waiting flatbed wagon. Luke followed, assisting the family's grandmother.

Happy squeals rose from the lot of the women. And did she even hear the baby's merry chortle? So much for stoic, cigar-store wooden Indians she'd been told to expect.

Luke and the porter returned. "That was so kind of you, William," Kitty said, loud enough for the conductor to hear that she knew the man's actual name. "Thank you."

The porter touched the brim of his cap. "Not at all, Miss Kitty. It's my job, Ma'am."

"Wait." She looked up into Luke's eyes. "Hey, partner. Got some change?"

Luke plunged his hand into his Marine dress pants pocket, then opened his palm. In the middle of the copper pennies gleamed a silver dollar.

William Marshall, Pullman porter, whose son graduated college first in his class, took a step back. "Oh, no. You already gave me an envelope for services rendered," he objected.

"This is to thank you for helping with the bags of my friends," Kitty insisted, nodding towards the women.

She took up the coin from Luke's palm. Why had she let her sister talk her into painting her nails? She flipped his silver dollar behind her while she still had sense of where William Marshall stood. She heard it land in his palm.

"Why, thank you, Missus. And Corporal, sir. You have yourselves a good visit, now!"

Even in her spectator pumps, Kitty had to look up to finally make solid contact with Luke Kayenta's fathomless eyes. The sight almost robbed her breath. "So," she managed, "How about a kiss?"

Luke smiled. She remembered how rare his smiles were. "I have many kisses for you, Kitty."

"You think you could plant the first?"

The small drama had drawn the attention of every remaining passenger on the train. She would have been mortified if he'd hesitated. But he did not. He swooped on her mouth as if it were his ultimate destination over the months they'd been apart.

Kitty didn't remember anything but the taste of Luke Kayenta after that, except for the vague sense of her skirts flying in the train's wake.

As Luke gasped for air, he buried his nose in her hair and her neck. He spoke a little. Not in English, but in that deep, nasal, drawling language of the people he was born into. As she felt her breasts rise, react against that buttoned-up uniform, the evidence of his own desire tantalized her thighs.

When they finally finished the kiss, both the train and the wagon were gone. Only a beat-up green truck remained at the station.

Luke's smile slid lopsided and his brow furrowed. "The silver dollar. It was for gas."

"Oh. Well, we can walk."

"But Kitty. I wrote to you, explained, remember? That we have many miles to go yet?"

She grinned. "Relax, Captain."

"I am not a captain in the Marines, Kitty."

"But you are still a member of the Office of Strategic Services? And that's your rank there?"

"Well, yes. That seems a hard unit of government to be released from."

"Then, in private, you're still my captain, who well earned his rank. There have to be some rewards for your service! So, my captain, if you've got ration coupons, I can pay for gas."

"You did not forget what I wrote in the letter, then, about distances here. You are teasing me. The women do that all the time. They say I am too serious."

She touched the slight stubble at his chin. "Luke. I'm so glad to see you. And this gardenia. Thank you. It's beautiful."

"*Saiah naaghai bikieh hozho, Yanaha,*" he said quietly, formally.

Kitty recognized the phrase from his letters. "Walk in beauty," was the poor English translation of the complex philosophy of life balance he explained in his letters. And he used the name he'd given her, Yanaha: She Meets the Enemy. His voice, even deeper than she remembered, made the name soar. Those exotic Valentino eyes were exactly as she remembered. Where had he found a gardenia? Its scent drifted past the strand of pearls against her throat.

She pressed her finger to his bottom lip. He drew it into his mouth. The sudden sensuousness of it robbed her breath. His arms closed around her again. She reveled in his familiar scent of corn and sage mixing with the oiled metal of his hidden firearm. There, encircled, she felt safe from the world and all its cruelties—from the petty aggressions of the railroad conductor toward the kind porter and the young Indian mother to the war itself.

"We need to go," Luke murmured into her hair. "The sun will not wait for us to finish."

"Finish what?" she teased him, now that she knew his other women did.

But he had no snappy comeback. He did not even grin or call her a brazen hussy.

"Drinking each other in," he answered her question.

Chapter 2

The Scotsman's Blanket

Propped up on the folds of his grandmother's blanket, Kitty's eyes, large and luminous, seemed out of balance, even frightened. Puzzled, Luke steered the truck around another dried-out ravine. Breathlessness joined her rapid-fire speech.

"Dom and Matty showed me pictures of Arizona, you know? From their schoolbooks. The pictures weren't like this. Like being here."

"There is more dust than in the pictures, maybe?" he tried.

"More sky, Luke. So much more sky." A trickle of sweat lined her forehead.

Did his home sicken her? "It would please my mother if we ate the peaches," he urged, trying to distract her from the wide-open sky he loved. "And my grandmother filled the canteen with water from a cottonwood grove. They say it is a sacred place. A ceremony place. Would you help me drink it, to honor her? And the place?"

16

Kitty opened the canteen, took a long swallow, then handed it to him. He smiled, seeing some color return to her cheeks.

"Almost as good as home's water," she said.

"She will be glad to hear that."

She winced. "When you tell her, don't say 'almost.' Our water comes from the Catskill Mountains. It is very good, healthy water, Papa says. From mountain snow melt. I didn't mean to sound, you know, ungrateful."

"You can tell her yourself, Kitty."

"Will she, will your mother and sisters and their kids...Luke, will they understand me?"

"They all speak and understand English."

"Yeah, good. But, well, when the train stopped in Wichita, I tried to order a sandwich. People there didn't understand a word coming out of me! And when I'm nervous, I talk even faster. Oh, Luke, do you think your family really wants—"

"They will not let me into their homes without you. Will you eat another peach?"

She snorted like his favorite mare. "I'm wearing the first one, thanks to this road."

"It looks good on you."

"Oh? Like a peach melba?"

"Now, you have me there."

"It's a dessert...peaches, raspberries, ice cream."

"It sounds delicious."

"No, it doesn't. You're not a dairy guy."

"Well. Most of it sounds delicious. Listen. I think we need to stop someplace."

"Where?"

"Eat," he urged. "They are from my mother's orchard. We should show the women they took good care of us on this journey, maybe." He raised his chin toward the section of an old leather belt hanging above the truck's door. "There is rougher road on the way. Hold onto the strap."

Kitty frowned, ignoring his direction, taking a chomping bite of the fruit. She did not like being ordered. No women did. Where was his sense?

He quieted his voice. "The strap is like the ones in your subway, yes?"

The mare snort happened again. "Aw, we've got rats bigger than these pebbles."

He laughed, half at her remark, half at his pleasure at understanding it right away. He was getting used to the speed, the cadence of her speech. She wiped her mouth with the back of her hand, then took hold of the strap. Peach juice slid down her chin, mixing its scent with hers. She had forgiven him, then? He hoped so. The sight of the juice made him think of other juices, the ones inside her that he wanted to help make flow.

He had to work harder at paying attention to the road as they approached the destination. The Navajo Service truck's hearty frame shook. "You brought boots?" he shouted over the rumble.

"Yes!"

"It is not a long walk."

"Walk? We have to walk to this place?"

"Yes!"

He stopped the truck. Dust now covered her hat and hair and the gardenia. But she was laughing.

"That was better than the bumper cars at Coney Island!" she proclaimed.

He grunted but could not hide his pleasure.

They sat on the truck's tailgate as he tightened the strings of his trail hat and replaced his Marine issue shoes with the high moccasins his mother had made for him. Easterners who toured the reservation in Mr. Harvey's motor cars wore boots like those Kitty Charante eased over her small feet.

She must have noticed his frown. "They're a present from Jack Spencer. Dude, huh?"

"Very much, dude."

"I declined the spurs that jingle jangle jingle. And I broke them in."

"Good."

There. The first mention of Jack Spenser and their work. Too soon. Luke did not like it intruding yet. He wanted everything beautiful for her.

He took out the folded blanket from its place stored behind her seat. This is my grandmother's gift to you. It is not one of her weavings. It is a gift from her mother. But she did not weave it either."

Kitty ran her fingers over the fine weave wool, its mixed red and black strands. "It's a plaid."

"Yes. It is very old, and comes with a story. A family story. My grandmother's mother told it to her. She gave me permission to tell you, even though it is not the right season for telling stories." Luke tried to find his storytelling voice, to honor his grandmother. Kitty's luminous attention helped.

"When my grandmother's grandmother was a small child, a snowstorm came up suddenly, when she was out gathering wood. It made her lost and confused her bearings. The storm got worse, the air colder. She came upon a creature she thought was a bear. But it was a man. A man with a pack on his back. The first White man she had ever seen. He was wrapped in furs and had a red beard. She was afraid of him, but he had kind eyes and seemed lost, too. He saw she was shivering, so he went into his pack and wrapped her in this blanket while they waited out the storm together.

"When the storm was over, my little long-ago grandmother led the traveler to her family. He was weak with hunger, so her mother fed him broth with a horn spoon. The family helped him find his way back to his trail. He gifted his little snow companion this blanket to thank her for guiding him to her people for their kind reception. The child's mother, in turn, gifted the red-haired stranger with one of her woven blankets to thank him for keeping her wandering child safe through the storm.

"My grandmother has cut a square from the blanket here, see? It is to be buried with her. The rest is for you, she says."

Kitty stared down at the neatly folded blanket and ran her fingers over its design. "Why? Luke, why does your grandmother give me such a gift?"

He shrugged. "You should ask her, maybe."

"It looks very old. But it's machine-made, I think."

"Yes. That's what they told us at the trading post. Made on a mechanical loom. That my little grandmother likely met a Scottish trader from the Hudson's Bay company called Big Jock. He must have been surprised that we had already been herding the Spanish churro sheep and weaving their wool for generations."

Kitty ran her cheek against the weave. "It's a wonderful gift. With a great story. But, Luke..."

"Yes?"

She looked into the summer sky. "It snows here?"

He laughed. "In winter, yes."

Luke placed the blanket over his shoulder, took her small waist between his hands, and helped her down to the ground.

He led the way. She took long, strong strides. They were in step, he and this woman who had started out together climbing the world's tallest building. A deep peace came over him as they walked, their fingertips touching.

"Where are we going?" she asked, a child's anticipation in her voice.

"To a place that reminds me of your home."

They reached the overlook as the setting sun painted the canyon and its ancient dwelling place with the rich colors of shade. The colors made it even more full of mystery. There. Kitty spotted the ruins. He handed her his binoculars.

"See? The Old Ones, they were city dwellers, like you."

"Old Ones?"

"The people long before us. Some call them the Anasazi."

"When did they live here?"

"Past memory, except in stories. Our neighbors the Hopi and the Pueblo people claim them as ancestors. Some say we, the newcomers, the Diné people, chased them here. Some say ghosts and shapeshifters roam the remains. They avoid this place."

"But not you."

"No, not me. I used to come to watch the animals who wander the canyons, make their homes here. But now, when I miss seeing you, miss the time we had together, I come. I imagine you there, see? In the middle of that long span? That is your street. You live halfway up—between your parents' and your sister's apartment. See that small room jutting off? The one with no windows, and a ladder to the hole in the roof?"

"Yes. I see it."

"That is the kiva of your father, his ceremonial room, where he goes to smoke his cigars and get away from all of you."

She laughed. "Yes, Pop would like it there!"

"And that lookout tower branching off the third story? That is where Matty and Dom can stand by, protecting the women."

"And play marbles with Yas and Nastas and Shandi?"

She was entering his dream of this place, Luke thought. Even better, she was putting her relatives together with his. "Yes," he encouraged her. "Why not? Everything is possible here, under this sky. It is the same sky as yours, Kitty."

"The same war," she said quietly.

"Yes. The same war."

She touched his sleeve. "You haven't done enough, suffered enough. That is why Jack stationed me here to finish my training. You're not only recruiting in your fancy dress uniform. You'll be going too. You'll be posted overseas, won't you? You'll go with your recruits—boys even younger than you are."

"I will go where I am told to go, Kitty. So will you. We are soldiers."

He slipped his arm around her waist. She leaned into his side. Yes, this is what he had been dreaming would happen between them over all the months of his shrine building.

Except that she was crying.

"Luke," she whispered. "I don't have your courage."

"Courage? If I had any courage, I would have asked you to marry me before now."

She whirled away from him.

He had done it. He had spoiled everything. "I am sorry. It is this place. Having you here, where I have dreamed of you. It is seeing you again. Forgive me."

"For what, you impossible man?"

"For not going to your parents first. Asking formally, learning the right gifts to bring, to suit the customs of your family, your religion, your people."

"Oh, Luke," she sighed the words out, then walked a few steps away.

The sun was gone over the horizon. She was gone, to a place deep inside herself. Was it a place that was always weeping for the loss of her husband, her child? Was that where she was now? Stop, he admonished himself. Stop questioning. Wait. Wait for her to come back.

Luke watched the first breeze of evening pick up the midnight dark waves of her hair. She turned. Her eyes were swollen.

"It is not about your gifts," she said. "It's about mine."

"I do not understand."

"Let's not try to understand any more today. Let's spread out your grandmother's beautiful blanket and love each other. Here. Now."

Luke stepped back. "Here? Now?" he repeated like a schoolboy.

She advanced. "Yes, Captain."

"But, we cannot."

"Why not?" She glanced to where the sun had been. "Will your family be worried at the delay?"

"No."

She tilted her head. "Luke, we could barely keep our hands off each other a year ago."

He remembered her up against that brick wall, still warm from the city's summer heat of the day. Were the shoulders under her beautiful clothes, dyed with one of the colors of the setting sun, still as rounded, as soft? "W-we agreed," he stammered out with nervousness, "in the letters, that our circumstances back then helped to fire our longing. We needed time to see if there was something true between us, remember?"

"Is there?"

"Yes, of course. But—"

"But?" she prompted, closing the small space between them, unbuttoning his uniform with those flashing red fingertips.

"I would not take advantage—"

She laughed. "Luke! Who is taking advantage of whom here?" she demanded.

Chapter 3

Culture Clash

How could he have forgotten how fast she could do this? His layers of clothing were no match for her.

When his shirt joined his dress blue jacket at her feet, she stopped abruptly. "The blanket!" she commanded.

He was trained to obey women when they used that tone of voice, so he pulled it from his shoulder, hoping he would not lose his undone trousers and even more face.

"Turn around," she commanded.

He turned, trying to keep all the reasons they should not do this in his mind. Count them, like a *bilagáana*, with numbers. They had the rules of her religion to consider. And what would his women think? And her father and brothers, surely, they would not approve.

Then there was her refusal to consider marrying him.

Go away from that one, reason number four. That one put a crack in his heart. Count. Count more.

But when he heard Kitty say his name and turned, and saw her, with her traveling clothes at her feet and her delicate white slip molded around her curves, he surrendered.

She'd shaken the blanket out and let it settle on the ground in the shade of a juniper tree.

He remembered to breathe. In. Out. "My grandmother called her blanket, Good Medicine."

"Beautiful," Kitty whispered.

"The women," Luke remembered his list, though he could barely make his mouth work to announce reason number five. "The women's hospitality will not permit—"

"...any more hesitation about using this gift," she finished for him.

She sounded so sure. Why had his women refused to accompany him to the railroad station? It was not their shyness, then? Or their welcome meal cooking schedule, or the need to make the children presentable to their guest, as they had said? None of that was why? Maybe they wanted this? The weakness of his joints when he looked at this woman he loved so deeply? He kneeled at Kitty's feet to help her remove the boots that carried the scent of New York City streets: bluestone, onions, gasoline, and the faint salt of the Atlantic.

His hands slid up the calves of her silk-covered leg as her fingers combed through his hair. It felt more right than rainfall, this insistent pull of their bodies. His fingers climbed until they found the edge of her stocking. He kissed the bare skin of her inner thigh. She unbuckled the stockings so that he could undress each leg slowly, savoring her moans of his name. Another manipulation, and the black, intricate spider web garment came free. Nothing else blocked his path.

Slowly, he felt his way inside her sacred woman's place. Deeper, making circles with the pads of his fingers, finding the spot that was hard, like he was on the outside. He imagined a rain-drenched canyon, full of secrets. This woman was rich in juices, in softness, in sound. In secrets. Her body trembled as she cried out and slid to her knees.

"Oh, love," she gasped out in a voice he had never heard from her before. "Oh, my sweet, sweet love." Was she well? Had he hurt her in his efforts? He took her warm face between his hands and was about to ask. But she pressed herself so close that he forgot the question.

Yes. It was right, her deep sigh breathed against his heart, resting. A good lover was one able to help his woman achieve her pleasure many times over. His grandmother, mother, and sisters had instructed him about this. So maybe they would not mind this delay in reaching the hogans. He slid the silk strap of Kitty's slip down with his nose. Enough to free a breast from its confines. To lick. To suckle. And then they were starting again, mixing her culture's kisses with Diné nips and bites. She laughed, yelped, and removed his remaining layers of clothing boldly. More boldly than he could think of being with her. He liked it very much.

But her hand gentled when it reached the whitened scars around his middle. Her voice deepened with compassion. "How well you've healed, darling boy."

He had not thought about the scars so much since Billy Zah had sung that first part of his Enemyway ceremony. He did not want her to think about them at all.

Did she sense this? Is that why she stroked his cheek, then kissed him slowly, firing his longing?

"Kitty," he whispered into her hair. "I want to be inside you."

She laughed. "You know what? I've been dreaming of that all year."

One of the reasons returned to plague him. Marriage. There should be no child from this if she did not want him as a husband. But he had not thought about what to do to prevent it.

He felt young, suddenly, and stupid. "Kitty, I have nothing to put over, to guard against. I have no—"

"Rubbers?"

That was the word, yes, he remembered the name from his basic training in California. And the light, leering way the sheaths were passed into the recruits' hands. "Yes, rubbers. I cannot protect you."

"It's all right."

"No, it is not."

She pressed two trembling fingers to his lips. "Luke, it's taken care of."

"Is it?" There were things women did. Of course there were. And he was ignorant of such things.

"Yes, sweet boy." Her laughter had a harsh edge this time. "Now help get me out of the rest, will you?"

She rose, spun away, gathering the hem of her slip and raising her crossed arms. The slip floated up over her head and cradled in the crook of her arm. She undid the clasps, and both breasts were freed. She stood before him in her full beauty.

She did not need help at all.

His gaze shifted to her feet, still in those dude boots. She was three years his elder. He was her sweet boy, who enhanced the pleasure she took at being a woman, an experienced widow. That was all, after a year of letters and gifts and friendship between their families. For a year, he had prayed to find the note of their first child's lullaby inside his flute, because he'd thought he was courting her.

Their cultures were so different. He could not even get that straight between them. Would he have to find his way to seeing Kitty Charante as lightly as she saw him? If he could, it would change who he was.

"Oh, God, Luke." She called him away from his thoughts. "Please. Look at me. What have I done?"

He raised his head slowly, past where she clutched her white silk slip between her breasts. To her eyes. "You're disappointed," she whispered. Tears spilled, streaking down her face.

"No, Kitty. Not in you. Never in you."

He reached up and took her waist gently, his thumbs circling very white skin. Another difference between them. He felt a scar of her own. He turned his head slowly, showing her his neck, like contrite Coyote in Diné stories she did not know.

He got to his feet then, and licked her tears, tasting loneliness, deep and abiding, the well of her sorrow. This beautiful, brave woman was giving him a chance to ease her loneliness. What kind of fool was he?

He lifted her in his arms, then placed her down beneath him on his grandmother's blanket.

"I am for you," he whispered in Kitty Charante's ear. He did not look in her eyes as he said the words that bound him to her. Because the world was so cruel, so uncertain. And he could not walk through it any longer without pledging himself to her.

She took his face between her hands. He thought she'd found him out, but there was only affection in those deep-set eyes. Not anger or pity. "And I am for you, my darling," she whispered, sealing their promise to each other in the way of the Diné.

He had tricked her into doing the last thing she wanted: marrying him.

How to tell her? He could not think of a way, not with her mouth covering his and the beautiful curves of her hips teasing, touching, circling his desire to join his body with hers.

"Come," she urged, as her hand guided him inside her.

Warm and wet, her woman's place pulsed. He would have to distract himself or he would compound the trouble between them by doing what he'd heard women complain of. His thumbs traced her hips. His hands squeezed her bottom. He thrust, then abandoned, then entered again. And again.

At first, she laughed at his comings and goings. Then her breathless invitations became higher-pitched demands. Finally, she anchored him to her when her legs crossed around his back. Her eyes fired as she closed her whole being around him. For him. For his delight.

If her anger had the same intensity, he was sure he would not survive it. He must remember to stay in her good graces, he thought as he collapsed, surrendering himself into the safekeeping of her arms.

Chapter 4
Family Circle

"At last," his sister said, swiping the last of Kitty's lipstick from behind his ear with a sigh. Luke felt the heat rise to his face. How did women find such spots, even when barely missed by his handkerchief?

Chooli's height almost matched his six feet. She wrapped her arm around his middle as they watched Kitty dole out gifts to his family. Born sixteen years before he was, Chooli had been his second mother for his whole life long. No position he achieved in the service of the United States would ever change her fierce circle of protection.

Would Kitty ever enter the circle of these women he loved?

"We do not mind that she's *bilagáana*. In case you were wondering."

He was.

She leaned closer to his heart. "But Adits'ah, she is wounded, like you. That can lead to affection and passion that is based on shared trouble."

She had used his sacred name, Adits'ah, He Understands. This conversation was important. Luke shrugged in the way he did when showing his horses that he was

34

harmless, approachable. "War is big trouble, sister."

"Well." She nodded toward two women—one as grounded to the land as a juniper tree, the other, his woman, two generations younger, her hands fliting like hummingbirds, perhaps not sure if she wanted to land at all. Chooli sighed. "We are used to big trouble here. Ask our grandmother about all she has lived through."

The woman in question, Anaba Bowman, was holding up the colorful French silk cloth Kitty had given her, draping it over her hands like a flowing waterfall. Luke's nieces and nephews surrounded them. Tiny Iris tugged at Kitty's skirt. She reached down, lifting the younger of Taswan's children in her arms, so Iris could see the dance of the cloth. What was this gift of hers? A handkerchief? Shawl? Something in between?

His mother and sister Taswan left their tea to brew in the kitchen and joined Chooli beside him. "Your Kitty is coming to us in the right way." Bly Kayenta observed in that deep, wise voice that had guided him all his life. "And she is good with the children."

"Not filling them with orders." Taswan, the smaller and sweeter-natured of his two sisters, agreed with their mother.

She'd said the word "orders" with disdain. All four of his women had prepared him, long ago, with that same tone for the orders he heard every day at boarding school. His women's simple directives concerning boarding school teachers: find out what they want, then give it to them. Then, when at home for holidays or for summer, be a free Diné again. Be a Bridge Person, for the good of the Diné. Chooli did not work in the kitchen of the boarding school anymore. She had only stayed on until he and Taswan graduated. And his eagle-eyed sister's own boys attended the new day school at Fort Defiance.

Kitty looked above the heads of the children around her. For him. He smiled and nodded when their eyes met.

"She is like that with the young ones of her family," he told his women.

"But has no babies of her own?" his mother asked.

"She lost one inside her, after the one who was her husband died."

"The airman." Chooli said.

Taswan nodded. "You helped him out of his life."

"Yes."

"We will help her to heal, maybe," their mother said. "Like we help you, suffering from the absence of the one born for the Salt Clan."

Nantai. His friend from childhood. He knew it was forbidden to say it, but Luke missed the sound of his clan brother's name. Missed since that day on the beach in Spain.

36

"Luke." His sister Chooli summoned his eyes. "It does not dishonor this woman's child, her man, that she carries you in her heart now."

"Does she?" he whispered, still seeing his failure, still seeing Nantai's boot on the sand. Kitty Charante enjoyed the pleasure they gave each other. But how could any woman love him?

"She does." Chooli's shoulder bumped his. She spoke close to his ear and said, "And not like that other *bilagáana*—the silly one who only wanted you to show off defiance to her people."

Another failure. They had patched his heart and body back together after that one's brothers had beat him bloody. Why did the women tolerate him at all?

"This *bilagáana* looks more like us. Acts more like us. And has a brave heart," Taswan, who was small, like their grandmother, and almost as mighty, assured him.

"And when did my still-young sisters achieve such wisdom?" Luke tried teasing them.

They laughed, then shoved him away from their company.

Kitty reached into her opened suitcase again. She pulled out baseball gloves for the boys.

***

The filmmaker, Dr. Colin Ross, shook his hand before they sat at the corner table of the elegant, potted palm-filled hotel cantina.

"Have you been enjoying your stay, my friend?" he asked.

"After Tiuana? Yes."

"Ah, of course. Tiuana is a backwater, without refinement. But we do what we must for the Fatherland. I have ordered you an El Diablo to celebrate your return."

Helmut Adler felt sickened by the very name. "I have eaten," he lied.

"The El Diablo is not a food specialty."

The waiter placed a tall glass filled with a reddish-purple concoction before him. "Most kind of you, Dr. Ross. But a glass of *agua fresca* will be more to my—"

"It is a tequila-based highball. Quite complex while refreshing. Sour lime, sweet black currant, and a fizz of biting ginger ale." He pushed the glass closer. "When in Mexico, one must adapt to the slow pace of the locals," his eyes became still, serious, "or risk standing out. Try it."

Adler took up the chilled glass with his good left hand. It slipped. He tightened his fingers before raising it to his lips. He drank. The blend of the tart lime, earthy sweetness, and subtle tequila slid down his throat, easing the annoyance he felt towards his Abwehr contact.

Ross smiled that same effortless, almost child-like smile that beamed out from all his film guides to exotic locations. "There. I believe I have a new convert to the Mexican Devil. Now, my friend, let us talk."

"I do not think my skills are being used to the greatest effect."

Dr. Ross tapped the onionskin pages set out before him on the tabletop made up of colorful decorative tiles. Their random placement distracted and annoyed Adler.

Ross nodded. "Yes. So, you have written, here in your report. So many words. More of a treatise than a report, perhaps?"

"Well, its subject matter is not "Around the World with A Movie Camera.""

The smile tightened. "Ah. You disapprove of more modern forms of communication?"

"Not at all," Adler backed off. "But I took some pains to detail the findings of my last assignment."

"And no one doubts your dedicated years in service to the Reich. Least of all myself, and those who are late to the party. But you know what they say about converts to a cause? We are its fiercest advocates and willing to give the last measure of devotion. Ah, Helmut. We are no longer young. And have fought in war already, have we not? This one has taken a toll on both of us. Your unfortunate adventure in New York suffered casualties." He nodded toward Adler's missing hand. "And did you know Mrs. Ross and I lost our only son during our invasion of the Soviet Union?"

"I did not," Adler lied. "My sincere condolences."

"So. Let us put all petty differences in style or taste aside, shall we?"

"Of course," Adler conceded to a grieving father.

"Now. Tell me what you have learned about the Americans' prison camp."

It was all there before the man, painstakingly typed with the fingers of the hand Adler had left. Had Colin Ross, who was better suited to propaganda than spying, even read it? Against his better judgment, Adler took another swallow of the fizzing concoction. It was subversive, pleasing. He wondered how much of its complexity was laced with tequila.

He began, "The prisoners, both Japanese and Nisei, are compliant. To a fault. At first, I thought it was for survival, or perhaps they thought that their stay was to be more temporary. But the Americans have been digging—they rerouted the Colorado River. This irrigation project of theirs is flooding dry land, creating farmland and gardens. The prisoners are feeding themselves. Even creating walkways over meditation rock gardens. Their young have found ways out of the camps—by men joining the armed forces, women joining the nursing corps."

"Can none be turned? Not even the ones conscripted into the military?"

"They are Americans, Dr. Ross."

"So are the members of the German-American Bund. I used to draw crowds of five hundred, one thousand of them to my lectures. I debated that anti-nazi Mayor of New York, to cheers!"

"That was praised on both sides of the Atlantic, *Herr Doktor*. But your visits occurred while the country was neutral, before it entered the war."

"Yes," Ross conceded, before burying his head in the pages again.

Perhaps he had read them and was fighting against the conclusions. Adler hoped he had not deflated the man's ego. He needed the arrogant blowhard. Helmut Adler had once commanded the admiration of Himmler himself. But his failures when he was among the sea wolves of the Atlantic hand landed him here, showing he was a good soldier, willing to follow orders from this showman-turned agent.

Ross was taking advantage of all the creature comforts of his Mexico City posting. He was a lightweight, a Scottish-descended Austrian, whose ideology shifted with the political winds. Even he admitted to that. He had been a proponent of democracy before he was a communist. A champion of the Jews, at least the ones who invested in his books and his films. Now he was as antisemitic as Goebbels. His latest lectures,

41

writings, and film work were all dutiful homages to the Third Reich.

But, despite his claims, despite his loss of a son who had not died in battle but was too stupid to take shelter from a storm and was struck by lightning on the Eastern Front, Colin Ross was no better than the American filmmaker Frank Buck, with his superficial travelogues to exotic lands. Playboys, the lot of them, appealing to the masses to enrich themselves, then changing with the wind. Now in his fifties, his fashionable light linen suit tailored to accentuate his trim form, he carefully placed Adler's report on the table and took a last sip of his Mexican Diablo before calling over their waiter to order two more. Adler opened his mouth to object, then realized his glass was indeed empty.

"I understand that the Poston War Relocation is located on the Colorado River Indian Reservation. And that was your point of infiltration, as your previous persona from the 1930s, your Professor Boerman, noted anthropologist?"

"Footnoted, perhaps. I knew better than to draw too much attention to my alias, who claimed to be a naturalized citizen of Chicago, a city full of humble German Americans."

"Taking advantage of a mongrel country full of discarded immigrants of the world. Well done."

Well, now, Adler realized. Was he entertaining the entertainer? He smiled. "A minor academic with few credentials. And my beard and dusty work clothes rendered me less suspicious among the Mohave tribe."

"Your decade in the American West has served you well. But there must be resentment from the tribes in the area of the camp? Resentment to mine for our purposes?"

"At first, yes, there was discontent. The camp was built against the wishes of the native council of the Mohave. But now, as their desert land is blooming, there is... well, appreciation. Of the irrigation. Tribe members are allowed to come inside the barbed wire, past the watchtowers."

"Ah. To band together with the Japanese and their descendants? In resentment of the government?"

"To play baseball."

"*Donnerwetter!*" Ross reached for his cocktail, swallowing a long drink. "This will be hard to explain to our superiors, Herr Adler."

"You might try corruption as a reason we cannot infiltrate."

"Yes, yes, that sometimes works." He returned his attention into the pages of Adler's report, fingers twitching against the paper. "And here, you have described the Mohave as a weak-minded people, drawn in by promises of freedom from a Jew-led government that has done nothing but oppress them. Ah, good, that is good for us.

A cause for our continued existence and use here in the New World, do you agree?"

Helmut Adler ignored the question.

His superior did not seem to mind. He sat back in his comfortable sling-backed Campeche chair. "The penetration here in Latin America is more successful, where the people are more used to strong men ruling them. Why, I believe we could take the Panama Canal by means of an airplane carrier close enough to drop one bomb...one! It would cripple canal traffic for a very long time. But, but...for now we must stay with the tasks we are given, and find favor with our friends across the Pacific."

"Yes, prove ourselves good partners of Japan. With useful information that will help them keep the Americans busy on their side of the world."

"Ah. Your specialty. The codebreaking. I have become well-versed on your exploits aboard our sea wolves, and your..." He glanced at Adler's right hand's prosthesis. "Shall we call them adventures in Spain and New York? Adventures that unfortunately did not bear the fruit that was hoped for?"

... And landed us both in this side show of the opera, Adler finished for him in his mind. For Dr. Ross was out of favor, too, traveling second class to Japan on diplomatic missions and spy side assignments. Assignments based in his popular film and book travels before the war. They were both in backwater status with the

Reich, a Reich busy with main stage exploits in Europe, Russia, and Africa. And intent to keep the volatile beast that was America focused away from Europe, and Hitler's stalled push to the east. Better for the Americans to concentrate their war efforts on trying to preserve their Pacific outposts from the Japanese onslaught.

They were both part of facilitating that side strategy.

"Fortunately, our Karl May novels-loving Führer has a warm place in his heart for you. Especially after your heroism's latest cost." Dr. Ross made another vague gesture toward his hand with its pincerlike metal fingers, part of a wonder of technologies developed for the maimed of the last war.

But Adler's injury was more recent. He ascribed it to his own underestimation of his adversary—a man who perpetrated a Spanish prison break of over one hundred Basque partisans as well as the deadly roof-mounted dispatch of five of the best Abwehr agents in New York.

But it was not Luke Kayenta who had maimed him. The truth was that his sliced-off fingers became infected, causing his hand to be reduced to a stump. A small woman caused it to happen. An American woman, born of the refuse of the Slavic nations that her country had welcomed as immigrants. He had misjudged that woman, badly, when he saw her only as bait for the Reich's true catch—her lover, the one who spoke in code.

He hoped Spencer's fetching switchboard operator with the stylish red shoes was dead, drowned in the waters off New York City, along with Luke Kayenta.

Dr. Ross drank the last of his El Diablo and granted Helmut Adler that full, guileless smile. "And now you are his embodiment of Old Shatterhand, of the Karl May Western novels, that our Führer loves, as if you'd planned it."

Chapter 5
Stars and Volcanoes

Luke was glad they'd traded his uniform and her formal clothes for soft wool shirts and trousers. Kitty's shirt and trousers took to her form with a dizzying effect. The children of his family led them outside to acquaint her with the chickens, sheep, garden, and horses. Then they feasted together on his mother's mutton stew made in the central hogan, where his grandmother resided.

Before the women settled the children into their sleeping spaces, his sisters shooed them out with a pack over Luke's shoulder. They walked away from the shadows of the hogans and past his mother's peach orchard. They made camp and a crackling fire before settling in to watch the quarter moon's rise over the mesas.

"Is the space out here easier to bear now that it is dark?" Luke asked Kitty.

"But it's not dark." The breathlessness was still in her voice. He wondered again if his home sickened the woman he loved. Slowly, she raised her head higher. "Luke, I have never seen so many stars."

"Not even on blackout nights in your city?"

"Not even then. There were still the shadows of buildings in the way. Here, it's all stars."

He reached for her hand. "And us. We are here. We are below them."

"Oh, look there, a shooting star!"

"Blow on it."

"What?"

"Hurry! Blow!"

She did. Had he seen the star too? Perhaps, out of the corner of his eye, while he was watching her. He blew on it.

She was staring at him. Of course she was.

He shook his head. "This is where I was a child. Where I was taught these things."

"Blowing out shooting stars like birthday candles?"

"Yes. To avoid troubles. We, the Diné, have many uh… guidelines." *Bilagáana* called them superstitions, taboos. He did not use those words. True, Navajo ways did not hold the same power over him as when he was a boy. But they were still part of being who he was. He would honor them, even if they made him strange to her, this *bilagáana* woman.

Kitty shivered. Was she cold? He built up the fire and settled back. She leaned against his chest. He breathed into her hair. Was she so swallowed by the night sky that she lost the feel of the soft night breezes, the smell of the Mexican pinyon trees, and his desire? He so wanted to kiss her.

She took hold of his sleeve, leaned her cheek against the soft, light wool of his shirt. He tried to see through her eyes. She was now a guest of his grandmother, in the world of his family, his clan, his people. Should she have gone to the place more like her own world first?

"Is it too much for you? Being out here? I can drive you to your training station at Fort Defiance tomorrow. There are more people, more buildings there."

She sat up and turned to face him. "Oh, no. Luke, not yet! Jack said I could report next week. You are my bridge. To your family. To here. To all of this."

He smiled. "Your tour guide? As you were for me in New York?"

"More than that. Oh, I was so awful to you when we first met! Say you forgive me. There's more now between us, isn't there?" The rapid-fire city speech was coming out of her.

He struggled to follow.

"Oh, Luke, please be patient with me. I will breathe easier in all this space, all this dry air. And your stars, leaving me down here, so small."

He took hold of her arms, now ridged at her sides. "Kitty. I do not think you are small. You take up all of my heart."

She looked stuck. Then those beautiful hands, with their flashing fingertips, took hold of his face. "Oh, love." She breathed out softly. "You must leave room for your marvelous women. And the little boys who follow your every move. And baby Iris, who laughs whenever she looks at you. They have been so generous in sharing you."

"You are the one who brought gifts."

Those fingers sifted through his hair. Went deeper into that sacred space, his scalp. He imagined his hair long and folded in the sacred way, in the tradition of his people. But that was not the way of his boarding school and college, or of the United States Marine Corps. Her lips were close to his ear. "Your women and their little ones, they gave me to you today. Oh, my darling. I think they don't even mind that I love you."

"You have love for me?"

She grinned wide. "Of course I do, you big lug."

He blinked. Lug. That was a good word, despite the blunt sound of it. She loved him. "I—" He stumbled. Tell her. Tell her what he had done. Tricked her. "Kitty, I—"

The howl echoing off the canyon suddenly brought her crashing against his chest. "What was that?"

"Coyotes." He smiled. "Bringing you down from the stars."

She glanced back in the direction of the women's hogans. "Will they come closer? Should we go back?"

"We will keep the fire high."

That was enough assurance. She eased herself into his arms and soon was opening her way to him easily under red fingertips. The smell of sheep lanolin and children mixed with her gardenia perfume as he covered them both with his grandmother's finely woven blanket.

She arched her back, bared her neck to him. He honored her vulnerability with a trace of soft kisses that lead a meandering trail to her secret places. She made soft, high notes of delight then. Three notes. Like a bird's trill. He would remember those notes. He would incorporate them into his flute's song. A courting song, for his wife. He would play it until she knew she was his wife. And had married him in return. In freedom, not trickery.

***

Michoacán, Mexico.

Ross handed him the binoculars. "Look! Only the upper portions of the main church are still visible!"

Helmut Adler observed the effect of the suddenly forming volcano, which had begun to rise out of a cornfield back in February. The town and the ruins of the San Juan Parangaricutiro Church were covered in lava and ash. The sight was now drawing both scientists and tourists from all over the world. And it had drawn two German

51

Abwehr agents over 300 kilometers from Mexico City to observe the beginnings of the life cycle of a volcano.

"My camera cannot capture this grandeur!" Ross said, as if he were narrating one of his travelogue films.

Adler sat, exhausted by the churning heat. "Well. Do your best." What he longed for was their return to the hotel. Its business was also booming, thanks to the bustling new tourist attraction. A beautiful hotel, converted from a Conquistador descendant's country palace. And yes, his companion, also no longer young, was loading his camera with his last roll of film.

That night, under the giant palms of the Mariposa, his companion was still waxing poetic about the newly forming earth drawing crowds of gawkers. "What are the words of the American song? 'Give me land, lots of land, under starry skies above?' Why do those people not understand? Our Third Reich is in the midst of colonial expansion to the east. Our leader's quest for *Lebensraum,* with breathing room for the Ayan Race, is much like the Manifest Destiny. After the war, all of the Americas will see how alike we are, I am sure."

Adler opened one eye. How much longer would he have to endure sunny lectures from his superior? Colin Ross's knowledge stretched the wide world over. But it was not deep. It skimmed surfaces, picked up whatever was on the wind. He was a tourist. Of places. Of ideas. What did he know of Americans, who had no real philosophy like theirs, born of thousands of years of struggle and refinement?

Well, at least the man knew a decent cocktail. Tonight's was a combination of local tequila, lemon, orange liquor, and soda water. Called a Daisy, it was sour, matching Helmut Adler's mood.

Ross raised his glass in salute. "I listened to our radio while you were enjoying your siesta, my friend. Our superiors and I have an adventure for you, Old Shatterhand."

Adler sighed, remembering again how this war was being helmed by a man who made sure frontline soldiers' provisions included Karl May's fanciful, fraudulent adventure tales of the American West.

"My friend. There is some very interesting information coming from Fort Defiance, in Arizona."

"Is there?"

"It began as trading post talk. About military recruiters coming on a certain Red Indian reservation."

Adler took a sip of his drink. He was unimpressed by the information. "This is nothing new. Recruiters come in every war, pulling out the young of their poor, to stand before our guns."

"Of course, of course. But they are going to the schools, this time. Finding the educated ones. Those few who can speak English in addition to their own language."

Adler sat up taller. "What language?"

"Navajo."

Adler's veins ignited. His Openshaw hand's metal fingers clicked together like a Geiger counter. He shifted closer to his superior and lowered his voice. "You were well-traveled in America throughout your travelogues and guidebook research, Dr. Ross. Did you make yourself familiar with these people, the Navajo?"

"My time there was limited. The languages of the area are not like those of the more civilized Red Indians. The grunts and glottal stop inflections are said to be impenetrable. And of course they developed no written symbols except strange rock carvings. Besides, the Indian schools beat their talk out of most of the children so that they remembered only English. I could find no interpreters among the local people. My efforts did not include a great deal of time in the American Southwest. Too much like the near east in desert land, without all the spectacular archaeological dream sites like Petra, eh?"

Adler had to keep himself from snorting. Poor excuses for the man's incuriosity! Enough of this. Time to pull rank on this subject. "I found two, Dr. Ross. Two of these schooled Indians."

"When you were Dr. Boerman? On your own American expeditions?"

"No. As myself. In Spain."

"Spain? These two men. Were they Navajo?"

"I am not certain," Adler admitted.

"How very interesting, my friend. These are the two Red Indians described in Himmler's briefings of your mission there?"

Damn Ross and Himmler both! What was the good of a secret intelligence agency that could not keep secrets from the lower ranks like this man? Well, never mind that Colin Ross knew the full extent of his failures. He might have another chance, even if it came through this fool.

"What have you heard?" Adler demanded, his pretense of respect eroding fast.

"Himmler thought of you when he learned that Japan needed us. Americans' new code, the one they are using in the Pacific. They are finding it impossible to decipher. Himmler congratulated himself for posting you so close to Mexico's border with Arizona. So, you think it might be of the Navajo people, this code?"

"Very possibly."

Adler thought of the enemy fire they were taking in the Argonne. How could they not understand what the Americans were saying? Where were they? Was there no way out of this hell? Perhaps Colin Ross had served, too. Think. Think strategically, without emotion.

"What do you propose we do?" Ross asked. "Can these Navajo be infiltrated?"

Adler smiled. There will be no *we*, he thought. And no infiltration. Not this time. Time to reverse their roles. "It must be stopped, before it can grow."

"Oh. Of course," his fellow agent agreed. "The expeditionary forces to each of the Japanese-held islands need two men to communicate for each military engagement. One to transmit, one to receive and translate. They will need many willing to do this, and under fire. Correct?"

Colin Ross was not as unintelligent as Adler had first thought.

"They are primitive people," Adler claimed knowledge he, in truth, did not yet have in detail about the reclusive Navajo. "Prone to many superstitions." That assertion always sounded correct. "I can use these beliefs to stop them. To turn them against these recruiters. Before this program can do extensive damage to our esteemed Far East ally."

Ross's eyes, Adler had learned, always scouted for winning possibilities and had become more animated.

"Let us work together on this, my friend. If successful, we can see both our places rise in the Reich."

Now, to take the reins more fully, thought Adler. "It will have to produce results quickly."

"Yes, of course. Time is of the essence." Colin Ross's grin widened. "Fortunately, my world travels have provided many sources of contact. Including a rather silly aging socialite widow that I met through Henry Ford, with whom I have a continuing correspondence. Her views on America First isolation have not changed. This widow is the proprietor of an exclusive Western resort in the area that is the object of our study."

"Resort?"

"A kind of spa. For the rich who wish to play at cowboy and Indian games while on holiday."

"I see," Adler said, although he did not understand at all.

"This widow would love to host an associate of mine, especially if he is an esteemed academic of quality, say, in diplomatic service?"

Closer. He was getting closer. "And I have spent most of the last decade as Professor Boerman," Adler said mildly. "With documents provided by an excellent engraver living in Mexico City."

The filmmaker pushed himself back from the table. "Well, then, we must leave our beautiful volcano and return, post haste."

An alliance with the soft, change-with-the-political wind travel writer? Yes, that was the way forward, Adler thought. And Colin Ross could remain comfortable in his Mexico City posting, with his tourist excursions to the valley of volcanoes. Comfortable enough to stay connected to Berlin, providing funds. That left the fieldwork position open. For him. He would cross the border into America. He would acquire revenge for the loss of his hand. And the humiliation that the Red Indian, Luke Kayenta, and his woman had caused.

Chapter 6

Sisters in Spirit

Kitty made her way through the peach orchard to the horse corral. She would soon be moving to Fort Defiance, as her communication training continued. But for now, she was grateful for this time with Luke and his family in canyon country, getting used to the sun, the stars, the altitude, and the landscape that were so different from her city life.

With their stealing away, being alone with Luke felt like the honeymoon she had never had with Philippe. Her heart was prepared for none of this...not the intensity of their lovemaking, the warm welcome and acceptance of his women and children, and this strange place where his people had thrived for hundreds of years.

His women's homes were like those of the Three Little Pigs, Kitty decided—the same six-sided shape but made of different building material. Each had a generous plot of land on the canyon floor. The four generations of households lived close to each other. Instead of on different floors of the same apartment building, their one-room homes were within walking distance, with carefully tended gardens and small orchards, corralled horses, sheep, goats, and their vigilant dog minders. His grandmother's hogan was built of the oldest material the Navajo used, clay. It had no windows. And yet it was large and held them all comfortably. Like her parents' apartment, Anaba Bowman's hogan was a central gathering place of the families of her children.

Luke's mother's hogan was built of rock. It contained four windows, so light filtered in throughout the day. So did a welcome breeze. Bly Kayenta's home centered around her cooking, with her large stove and cooking pots hanging on display like fond children in a family portrait. And in the sunlight coming through one window was a carefully nurtured Gardinia plant, solving the mystery of how Luke had acquired the blossom for her mauve suit's corsage.

Taswan's home was built of well-placed logs. It had windows in all its six walls, and modern conveniences inside to match. Both Taswan's and Chooli's husbands worked for the railroad, maintaining and securing the lines. They were away much of the time, working up and down the Santa Fe line, keeping it in good repair for all the increased wartime traffic. Kitty was glad the two men had each other for company. Her father and his brother had worked on the New York Central together. The whole family had celebrated when Uncle Janko was promoted to brakeman. But that was only weeks before he was crushed to death when he fell between trains. She could tell Luke's sisters worried about their husbands' safety too, as they 'God blessed' them within their children's bedside prayers each night.

Only the saddle-shoe-wearing older sister Chooli no longer lived in a hogan. She and her lively sons stayed with their mother and Luke when visiting. Chooli and her husband had recently purchased a house in town. Living there allowed Chooli to work at the telegraph office. Like Luke, she had her feet firmly planted in both worlds—that of her Indian neighbors, and the faster-paced one of the Anglo-American culture around the Navajo and Hopi.

Sleeping quarters in each home were partitioned by the women's beautiful woven rugs. And each household had a large, upright loom set up outside, close by the eastern-facing door. There were two looms outside Taswan's hogan, one a little higher to suit her older sister's height. Kitty noticed the differences between the women's weavings, highlighting the passions of each artist. Taswan loved carmine-colored birds, while Chooli favored bold geometric patterns. The older women, Luke's mother and grandmother, also wove blankets and saddle blankets for the families. These mixed cotton strands with wool relied less on dyes but tones of shifted whites, blacks, greys, and browns, according to the color of the sheep that had provided the wool. All the women's looms were a business too—they provided rugs to sell to tourists at the trading post.

Kitty walked past the homes for her early morning time in the orchard. From there she could watch the horses from her usual distance. She composed a letter to her parents in her mind as she walked almost silently in the moccasins Luke made her.

Mama's a city girl, born and bred, but you, Papa...you told us about your home on a remote island in the Adriatic Sea, rich in olive groves and honey. How could you bear to leave a place as beautiful as this?

She longed to get closer to the fenced-in horses but stayed under the shade of the peach tree. Then, without warning except for the slight breeze sending his scent of juniper and leather, Luke was beside her. His large, gentle hands slipped about her waist. *To be continued, Mama, Papa*, she thought, and she nestled further into his hold.

They watched the herd together. In silence. Kitty was getting used to his silences. In this wide-open territory of his homeland, she was learning new things about him. That he lived in those silences. Lived fully, part of this landscape she'd first thought barren and unforgiving, but now she realized was full of life.

He was full of life, a life he wanted to join with hers. How could she bear to tell him there was no future for them beyond this glorious present? Luke's posture went even more loose, as if he'd sensed her growing unease. His chin pointed toward his mother's horses. "Watch, Kitty. They are communicating with each other."

"How?"

"With feelings. They are talking feelings all the time."

"What feelings?"

"Well, look at that cluster. How they swish away flies."

"All right..."

"Yuma, he is the brown Pinto. See the rhythm to his tail? He is the live-and-let-live type. The flies? They are just part of the music of life to him. Niyol is that light Cayuse pony. She whips them off her side—very dramatic."

Kitty laughed. "How dare they bother her."

"Ai!" He laughed. "Yazhi is the white-backed Paint. See her?"

"Yes."

"She swishes and also stomps. She is a guardian. She wants the herd to know that there are bad flies over here."

"Well, I like her. I'll stay clear of that corner. She's talking to us too."

"Yazhi will like you, I think. You should get to know her better, maybe."

"Oh, Luke. I don't know."

"Those dude boots of yours. They should do more than kick up dirt. They should meet the warmth of a saddle."

"It's not the saddle that makes me hesitate. It's having Yazhi underneath."

"She will recognize a sister in spirit. She will welcome your company on a ride today, maybe." He took her hand. "Let's talk to her about it."

"But I don't speak horse."

"I will translate for you. There, now, see? They are herding, like the sheep."

"I don't understand."

"What? Do they not look like a herd of New York City's taxi-cabs? You round those up nicely with your whistle."

"Why, Luke. You're teasing me."

He grunted. "Do not tell my sisters humor sometimes visits me. I must preserve my serious warrior image."

As they walked around the corral, Luke spoke even more slowly than usual. For her? For the horses? For both?

"In our stories, the sun rides a horse as white as Yazhi across the sky and keeps some at places in each of our directions. They are the colors of the morning, noon, afternoon, and evening."

"Like these horses."

"Yes, like these. They know me."

"But not me."

"They are wary of you, but curious. They are thinking. Slowly. Ready to run, if you are dangerous."

"If I'm dangerous? Look at the size of them!"

"But we are the predators. They are prey animals, Kitty. Watchful. Fast. Always ready to flee, if a panther approaches, or a whirlwind."

"Whirlwind?"

"Yes. Swirls of dust that come up from the ground in dry summers, like this one."

"Dust devils making tumbling tumbleweeds?"

"That is how White people see them, yes. To us they are more sacred. Part of hero stories. Part of our art, with the symbol of whirling logs. Swirling one way, they are full of blessings from Yei, the spirits of good people gone before."

"And the other way?"

"Chindi. Restless. Leftover evil from lives lived. To our horses, whirlwinds are sudden, and full of sound. Dangerous, startling. See how even now, when it is calm, the horses look out for each other. Nervous. Watch their ears. Niyol, Yuma, and Doba, the curious Mustang—they are pointing ears backwards, sorting you out, concentrating, ready to let the rest of the herd know if you are a danger. But your friend Yazhi. Look. Her ears are perky, and her head is high. I think she cannot wait to meet you."

The white backed horse left the company of the others and approached them.

The horse was even more beautiful up close. "Luke. How did you know?"

"That she has good taste in women? That is not difficult to translate. Move slowly. Your hand to her nose. Yes, love."

Yazhi nodded, sniffing her fingers.

Kitty laughed softly. "She likes Gardenia cologne."

"Smell her in return."

"Where?"

"At her snout."

She did.

"There. She is happy that you like the smell of Horse. Want to ride?"

"Oh, Luke."

He cocked his head, just like the horse. "She is asking, not me."

Chapter 7

New Women

"You honor the young ones," Taswan said quietly.

Kitty tightened the straps of her backpack across her shoulders. "Sure. Yours and Chooli's kids are great, funny, full of spark."

"Spark?"

"Energy. You know? Like lightning? Spunk?" Kitty tried.

Taswan's look of confusion changed. Her mouth burst open with a wide smile, like her grandmother's smile. She left Kitty's side and skipped up to her tall, older sister, who was further along on the trail. "See? Luke's woman understands better than we know. Better than she knows, maybe."

Chooli's eyes looked back at Kitty, remaining wary.

This hike they'd invited her on was the first time she'd been alone with Luke's sisters. They'd told her to pack a swimsuit and towel in her knapsack, so she thought they'd be going to a lake or creek for a dip, which sounded fine to her. It was also the first time she'd been without the energy of their children dancing around them. Today, the boys were herding the sheep under the watchful eye of their uncle. Luke's mother and grandmother were already outside in the dawn's light, Bly Kayenta weaving a beautiful rug on her loom while Iris slept in her basket between them.

But this morning, Luke's sisters—grown, capable women, were not doing something that provided for Luke's extended family. That's how Kitty had always seen them before this, she realized. But now the three of them were walking in the early morning, on empty stomachs, without even a good jolt of coffee. Walking through a cottonwood grove dappled in the light of the rising sun. They'd not even spoken until this strange conversation about children.

All of it made her nervous.

The walking wasn't hard. Even though there was no path that Kitty could see, the sisters seemed to know where they were going.

"Look at that one," Chooli, who was in the lead, said quietly, with reverence, before she stopped. Both sisters seemed to find the object of her affectionate tone.

But Kitty kept staring through the trees. One what? A bird? Were they birdwatching? No. They were looking further down. A rabbit scampering along the ground, maybe?

"These are cottonwoods," Chooli explained patiently.

Taswan left the path her sister was making through the woods. She looked over her shoulder. "Look, Kitty—six trunks!"

She smiled. "Two for each of us."

"Yes! Two for each of us to spread our arms between."

They looked at her expectantly. "Uh. Okay," Kitty said.

Chooli followed her sister, so Kitty followed Chooli. The older sister stood beside the tree at an arm's length from her sister and stretched her arms between two of the tree's trunks. It seemed instinctive, like what Kitty did when she entered St. Michael's and dipped her hand in the Holy Water font, or knelt before she entered a pew. So, she followed suit and stood an arm's length from First Sister, as Luke sometimes called Chooli. The sisters' arms stretched out then, and linked with each other, then with her. They had formed a circle around the tree.

Chooli and Taswan looked up into its branches, so Kitty did too. The silence intensified. Then a breeze came up to rustle the leaves. Both sisters closed their eyes, took in three deep breaths. They squeezed Kitty's hands before they let her go.

"We are on the right path," Chooli proclaimed quietly.

Taswan giggled. "If you say so, Medicine Woman."

They left the company of the tree and continued their hike. Kitty didn't know what just happened, but she was grateful for it. She was finally relaxing in the company of these young women who Luke loved, as her own mother would say, "beyond the beyond."

Taswan walked closer to her side. "We believe that trees with many trunks, like that one, are as beautiful as the others but more...sacred. Yes, I think that is the right word. I teased my sister because she led our... appreciation of the tree, in a way that is usually the way that some of our men do. The men we call Singers."

"Priests?"

"Yes. Like priests. Priests and doctors put together."

Kitty nodded. "Yeah, they're mostly men where I came from, too. Good for Chooli. We know what's holy, too."

Chooli did not slow her long-legged stride, but grunted, like her brother sometimes did.

The vegetation became greener and lusher as they walked, and soon they were sifting themselves in between its density. Or, rather, the sisters sifted through, Kitty struggled, with branches grabbing at her hair and sleeves.

But soon the reward was before them.

"Wow. That's some swimming hole," Kitty said.

"Yes. To swim. But first, we say thanks for allowing us to find this place."

"How?"

"With gifts. Did you bring the cigarettes?"

"Sure." Kitty released her knapsack from her shoulders, then dug around until she found the pack of Camels from the carton Jack Spencer had insisted that she pack to "keep on the good side of any Marines you come across." Wait till she tells him that it was a couple of Navajo women who had first requested them.

Taswan didn't light up but quietly opened the cigarette before placing the threads of tobacco on a flat rock. It was soon joined by corn pollen from the pouch around her neck. Chooli's contributions were a braided stiff palm-like substance that she called sweetgrass, and leaves that smelled like Thanksgiving at Mama and Pop's apartment—sage. The sisters carefully placed their items on the rock, and then looked to her again.

"A light?" Chooli asked.

"Sure." Kitty provided another of her boss Jack Spenser's essentials: a red Parker compact that burst into flame at a flick of the thumb. Soon, the sage bundle was lit like a cigar and wreathing the rock and its offerings in white smoke.

"There, Chooli pronounced, mounting the smoking sage against the little mound of corn pollen. We have paid our respects. Now we can enter the spring."

They each leaned over and felt the temperature. Cool. Refreshing after their hike, Kitty thought as they removed their sandals.

Taswan looked up from her task. "It is beautiful to you, this place? You, who swims in the wide ocean?"

"Very beautiful," Kitty assured them. "And a lot more peaceful."

It wasn't peaceful for long. Once they'd peeled off their outer clothing they jumped, shrieked, and splashed each other so that if she closed her eyes, it seemed like a summer day with her family at Coney Island. Kitty swam the circumference, dove deep. She emerged to find the sisters watching her with relieved looks on their faces.

"What a great dip!"

"You like it underwater," Chooli observed in a voice that trembled.

"I always did. It's another world down there."

"Where you breath like Frog."

"Well, I've got lots of lungpower. Hey." She pushed the dripping hair back off her brow. "Were you worried about me?"

"Not anymore," Taswan assured her. "How do you feel?"

"Like a new woman."

The sisters exchanged glances again. Not worried, this time. But wide-eyed. Awed.

"Okay, spill the beans, you two. What did I do this time?"

"You named it, Kitty," Taswan whispered.

"Named what?"

Taswan looked to her elder sister, who shook her head. "What we invited you to do with us. It's a...well, it was something like a ceremony, our hike," she explained.

"Oh? The whole hike?"

"Yes."

"So, this ceremony, it's over with our dip? Before I even knew it started?"

"No."

"Not yet," Taswan added.

"So, what do we do now?"

"We sit. We wait."

"For what?"

"We wait," she said again, shaking out her towel, placing it on a slab of pale salmon sandstone, and sitting on it. Her sister walked a few feet away and did the same. Kitty followed suit, leaning back on her elbows in the warm sun.

"What if—"

"We wait," Chooli insisted quietly.

Her sister let out a giggle, sounding like her little son.

Kitty shrugged. "Okay, okay. We wait."

Kitty was enjoying the sun on her face when a soft sifting caught her attention. She opened her eyes in time to see a dozen butterflies swoop around Chooli's shoulders as if the beaded wildflowers she had sewn onto her shawl were a meadow in summer. Kitty blinked twice to make sure they were real. And in that time, they were flying off again.

"Well," her younger sister said quietly. "That was quite a gaggle!"

Choolie grunted. "A flutter. It's called a flutter. I must study this."

"That's exactly what you must not do. You already know the message of the butterflies," Taswan insisted. "Walk light. Dance more."

Chooli hugged her knees. "I will consider this."

"Good."

At that moment, Kitty watched a salamander emerge from under a rock and climb over the toes of Taswan's bare foot before disappearing into a patch of grass.

"Oh," she responded. "Hello, little one."

"Little self-healer, growing her own tail back," Chooli continued, nodding. She raised her head higher. Kitty knew that look. Her eight-year-older sister, Ana, used it often on her. "Maybe you should be making your own teas and poultices, not running to our mother's hogan for a remedy when you or your babies are feeling poorly, sister."

Bingo. Kitty realized what their guidance to each other was based on. She laughed. "That's what we were waiting for? Visits from an animal? For advice?"

"Yes. We gather the animals," Taswan said. "I'll weave salamanders into my next rug, I think. And Chooli will have fun putting her butterfly flock into her next watercolor painting."

"You paint, Chooli?" Kitty asked, trying to imagine Luke's practical sister sitting before an easel.

"Yes. Don't you?"

"I—no. I mean I doodle cartoons in my letters home."

"We are all artists. Let us be quiet now. And wait. For you."

"I saw fish when I dove down on our swim."

Taswan's eyes were hopeful. "What kind of fish? What did it look like?"

"They already know you as one of them," Chooli dismissed the idea, sounding more like Kitty's sister, Anya, by the minute. "Those water beings want you to teach our brother. They were for him, and the other Diné men who are becoming Marines. You must wait for your own messenger. Be still now."

But it was difficult as the minutes ticked by. Maybe this only happened for native women. Maybe she would never be able to match the beautiful, accepting stillness of Luke's sisters. At home, Kitty still fidgeted during Mass.

Then the morning quiet was broken by a soft rustling in the vegetation. A stumble, a halt, and Kitty was eye to eye with a blinking colt. Her breath caught. She held it in her throat. The little face came closer, nudged her shoulder like a scratching post, then stumbled on toward the water for a drink.

In the distance, a call. The foal picked up her ears, turned, and disappeared in the greenery again.

Both sisters sat higher. "Well," Chooli decided. "We can head back home now."

"I can almost smell Grandmother's fry bread."

"Wait," Kitty. "Was that little horse for me? Where did he come from?"

Taswan laughed. "He was a she, I think. A mustang. They are wild but sometimes visit. And of course she came for you, Kitty."

They were slipping into their clothes again. Kitty scrambled to do the same. "But what does it mean?"

"That you should study the horse, like you study our brother, who loves them."

"But I can't ride." She'd barely touched beautiful Yazhi.

"And he can't swim. Yet." The sisters began combing out their impossibly long, shining hair. They placed the mass in the palm of their hand, then began wrapping it in a double bun with a long strip of wool. As they finished, Taswan placed her backpack on her shoulder. "You should bring Luke here, maybe. We will allow it, even if it is sacred to women. He is a man good to women."

"Good for women, too," Chooli chimed in. "Yes, Kitty?"

Both sisters dissolved in giggles and then ran up ahead of her, their heads together.

Soon they were walking through the cottonwood grove again. Kitty saw it differently now. It was the same. But she was a new woman. She watched the straight backs of the sisters as they walked through the dappled sunlight. Kitty knew that Luke loved both of them with his whole heart. But he was more protective of Taswan, who was delicate and small, like their grandmother. It was that sister who walked more slowly until they were pacing shoulder to shoulder.

"Luke is stuck, Kitty."

"Is he?"

"Yes. I think he killed someone in the water. Did he?"

Kitty saw herself slashing through the hand that was trying to pull Luke into the depths. It was she who killed the Nazi spy, who pretended to be the Chicago anthropologist. "I'm sorry, Taswan. I'm not supposed to talk about that."

"Yes. I understand. But my brother must be remade. In a ceremony. Like yours today, only for warriors. We arranged for one. It is called an Enemyway. But he did not complete it. The other warrior's family. They came. Showing respect. Showing that they did not hold our Luke responsible for the death of his clan brother. Still, he did not complete the ceremony."

"No?"

On the first day they'd met, Luke said goodbye to his friend who died in Spain, Kitty remembered. He'd let corn pollen drift into the wind from the observation deck of the Empire State Building. Was this ceremony Taswan spoke of related to that one? There was so much she needed to know about how Navajo people saw the world, and their place in it.

"What he needs is not on our mesas," Taswan continued. "Not among the trees or fields or in the desert. Maybe here, in water, the evil that plagues him remains. It still has a hold on his heart. He must swim through it, I think."

"Swimming is a good skill. For everyone."

"Even desert people?"

"Everyone."

"Well. Some of us cannot swim. And our children are playful in the water. They will need two teachers, maybe? You and Luke? What do you think?"

Kitty smiled. Luke's shy sister knew how to get her point across in her own roundabout way. And didn't Kitty's own brothers become better swimmers after they'd taught her?

"And then, when this is accomplished, we can dance," Chooli said, joining their conversation. Now the sisters flanked her.

"Dance?"

"Yes. We arranged that part of his Enemyway Ceremony—the Girls Dance. We bought gifts for everyone, hired a singer, set aside the place, and the time." The annoyance was still in her voice.

"Then our Luke." Taswan picked up the story, sounding more sad than angry, "he disappeared."

"Oh."

"We did not know why he was so shy around this part of his Enemyway Ceremony."

"We hosted this Dance. Everyone came. We want him back, whole, after meeting the enemy, after his clan brother did not come back. But this part, connecting to the female, being chosen as protector of women, of children, of our Mother Earth. But Luke said he thought he heard wolves that night and could not leave the sheep."

"What happened?"

"We sent away the Singer."

"The Medicine Person, the... priest," Chooli clarified.

Taswan smiled. "We had a dance party instead."

Chooli grunted. "Your being here honors us, Kitty. We want our brother, our son and grandson, our children's uncle restored to us. So, we ask you to choose him."

"Choose him?"

"Not forever!" Taswan hastened to assure her, casting a stern-mouthed look at her sister. "In the dance. The Girl's Dance."

Her sister frowned. "We think it was because of you that he spent that night with the sheep. We think he was waiting for you."

"To choose him, in the dance. So that this last part of the ceremony can be completed. Will you choose him, Kitty?"

Both stopped walking. They took each of her hands between theirs.

Two formidable sisters against one. Well, Kitty thought, she should be happy his mother and grandmother were back at their hogans, minding the babies. "Yes, of course," she gave up. "We have already danced in my city. At the Savoy, uptown."

"Oh, we know. He has taught us these dances," Taswan said.

"The Lindy Hop, the Peabody," Chooli continued as her mouth widened in a smile. "We like them very much."

***

It was almost having Lander and Yuli back, the faithful shepherding dogs who had worked with Luke in Spain and become his friends. Those friends gave up their lives for his. Their faithfulness still haunted him. He had not properly said goodbye, mourned them, with all the things that followed soon after.

These two herding dogs, Bina and Yiska, were performing their duties with the flock's yearlings. These dogs would never allow Luke to be theirs. They had already given their loyalty to his two older nephews. They were good companions and rounders for his mother's flock. And they found lost lambs

80

well, his nephews assured him. Luke smiled. They were certainly considering four-year-old Teddy and toddling Iris as additional yearlings to be kept in line.

Luke wondered how his own Code Talker lambs were doing. He was proud of the first class recruited, then sent off to San Diego for training and study. They had worked together well, just as he and Nantai had in the mountains of Spain. The words they'd agreed upon without letter-corresponding-code were familiar, from their lives. A submarine was *besh lo*, iron fish. A battleship was a whale, *lo tso*. A bomber plane was a *jay sho*, buzzard, dropping *ye shi*, eggs. Of course, Our Mother, *Ne he mah* was America. Together, they'd expanded their code words so that the often-used letters had more than one Dine reference word. Nothing was written. Their blackboards were only used for their radio studies. They learned about those vital instruments too...how to use them and do simple repairs. All of the twenty-nine volunteers, from the boys he suspected were not yet eighteen to the overage thirty-three-year-old Carl Gorman, who had the strength and stamina to carry those heavy radios, too.

Why had the Marines left him behind when the class was shipped to Guadalcanal? To recruit and teach the next group, they'd said. But were there other reasons they found him unfit for active duty? Was it only that he was a Marine who could not swim?

Did they still worry about his mind not being in the right place for war, as the O.S.S. had after Spain? Was that part of Kitty's visit? Was her assignment something beyond finishing her own communication training at Fort Defiance? Did she also report back to Jack Spenser and the Office of Strategic Services? About his fitness to hold the secrets of the code deep in his heart?

Luke did not like the poison of suspicion that crept behind them as they lived among his family. The suspicion was only banished from his heart when they loved each other. He sometimes wanted to live in those pure moments of sensation of joy as their bodies danced in endless figures of love. They stole those moments often, with eager anticipation before, with sublime exhaustion after.

They'd loved each other in all his favorite places, places he'd longed to take her over the months they had been apart— in the shadow of the high red and orange cliffs and sandstone bluffs, among the pine and his family's grazing sheep.

His fingers longed to make the sounds of the instrument he'd carefully packed away.

His women called him a bridge person, a person of two worlds. All he knew was that he did not belong here anymore. This place that he loved was letting go of him. Again. As it did when he left for his schooling, and again when he'd entered the federal wartime service with the O.S.S.

He was now a stranger, a visitor in his own country. Because he was a warrior, in service. So that his nephews, and Kitty's, and all the children of the canyons, both here and on Manhattan Island, would not have to go to war to defend the mother of them all—the land.

But his father and grandfather said the same about the last war, the one that was supposed to end them all. Its effects had only ended the lives of the two men he loved before he had a chance to ask them so many things. About themselves, about the history of the Diné.

His little niece wound her finger in a circle of lamb's wool. The lamb, startled by her cry, ran off with Iris in tow.

"Baby's caught!" her brother alerted him.

Luke ran. He tackled the lamb. Teddy joined the effort and helpfully sat on the yearling as Luke unwound the knot of wool from his niece's thumb. "Are you Coyote after Rabbit, Iris?" he tried to soothe her cries as he checked her remaining fingers for injury.

"She was! She was, Uncle!" Teddy decided. Iris's cries turned to laughter. Luke breathed easier. "Good guardians," he complimented her brother and the dogs Bina and Yiska.

"Chase us now, Iris!" Teddy and the dogs demanded with their play bows and wagging tails.

"Luke scooped his niece into his arms. "Against your longer limbs and these four-leggeds? Is that fair?"

"She is small! She can find a hole, like Rabbit in the story," Teddy countered.

His nephew knew stories already. Luke shook his head at the wonder of it. He'd missed too much of these young ones' lives. Iris rubbed her nose and cheek against his shirt. He knew that sign. She needed her mother's breast. But then her small hand touched his cheek. It was for him, this sign of affection? He rocked his body, shifting weight from side to side. The three notes he'd stolen from Kitty's voice came out of his mouth. Iris responded. She dug her way deeper into his hold. He softened the notes, and her eyelids drooped. The lullaby, a spell song, was working!

He watched Teddy explain which dog would now play Rabbit in the story. When Luke was a child, the men would smile when he asked them about how things came to be. 'It's in the stories,' they would tell him. Did they believe it? Or were they waiting for him to become older before they linked the stories of the four worlds, and emergences to migrations, to history? What did their own grandparents tell them about the Long Walk and the years of exile at Bosque Redondo? How had they convinced his mother and grandmother to marry them? And how did the wider world seem to them? Did it throw

84

them as far out of balance as the world beyond Dinètah did to him?

He looked down at the beauty of his sleeping niece. He needed to be out of his own thoughts more. He needed to love living here in the present, like these young ones did.

"You have put away your flute."

His mother was beside him. His Marine-issued binoculars metal clicked, sounding against her necklaces. The smell from the frybread basket at her hip reached his senses. He gave out a small burst of laughter to hide his shame. "I may someday be a better musician than I am a sheepherder. I did not hear you."

"My son," she said in that way when she'd caught him trying to change the subject. "You are not worried about squeaks in your instrument."

He shrugged, then gave up his grieving heart to her. Here. In this present moment. "She will not have me."

"Your bodies say something different."

"For life, I mean. Our lives, together."

She looked out over Teddy and the herd for so long that he thought she was finished with the subject of his love life. But then she touched his back. "It is hard to think of a future when at war. Your father and I felt this way over the time of the last one. Still, our wonderful surprise after we thought our family was complete—you—came to us after the fighting, and the Spanish flu sickness took away so many. You, a bridge person, who we named for one of the *bilagáana* holy writers, whose book is full of angels. You were our assurance of the future."

"Do you think this is Kitty's way? That she cannot think of the future?"

"Maybe."

"I could bear it then. I cannot think this way myself, but I could bear it."

When his mother leaned over and nuzzled the top of Iris's head, the baby woke, smiling. Soon, both she and her brother's eager fingers were tearing off pieces of their grandmother's gift of frybread.

She watched him feed Iris. "You were looking for a baby's lullaby in your flute."

"Yes. I want to be seen as worthy of that in her eyes. But in her time. When she is ready. And I fear she will never be. That is what her eyes tell me."

His mother frowned. "Her eyes speak to you, then, great knower of women? She raised his binoculars to her own sightlines. "She returns with your sisters," she announced while he could see only specks on the horizon. "Come inside for breakfast, Teddy," she summoned her grandson. She put her bread-laden basket into Luke's hand. "Here," she said. "Feed both her hungers."

Kitty lifted her arm in a wave. Luke was waiting for them outside his family's hogans. He held his laughing little niece in one arm, and his mother's or grandmother's fry bread in the other. He'd flung a towel over his shoulder, like the first time he'd offered the treat that her own mother now made regularly in her own way, smothered in maple syrup.

How Kitty loved being the cause of his smile. She was falling hard, too hard. And in wartime. With another crazy, fearless man. Would she ever learn?

***

"I have found you a Winnetou, Old Shatterhand!"

Adler frowned. Do not do that, he admonished himself. It made Ross worse. Smile instead.

"Professor Boerman? Meet your guide in the Land of Enchantment—Toby Wheeler."

Beside Colin Ross was a lean, dark, slack-jawed man in his forties, below average height, but with broad shoulders. His nose bore the look of being broken more than once. Half of his face had a light, grizzled stubble. But the other side was as clean-shaven as an adolescent. It gave the impression that he was always in the shadows. He came out of those shadows now, doffed his beaten felt hat, and made a small bow.

"'Between La Junta in Colorado and Los Angeles in California there lies a journey which, in connection with its side trips, is unequalled!'" he proclaimed. "Why? 'Because there is only one Grand Cañon, one Pike's Peak with its adjacent wonderland, and because, as a rule, elsewhere in the United States—or in the world, for that matter,—forests do not turn into stone nor stars hurl themselves into the earth with a force that buries them too deep for resurrection.'" He bowed again. "My papa used to read to me nightly from Miss Whiting's travel book!" he proclaimed.

Colin Ross pressed his hands together in a single clap. "Ah, yes. *The Land of Enchantment, From Pike's Peak to the Pacific*! Delightful rendition, Mr. Wheeler! I know the book well. It inspired me in my American travels. I have always had the desire to include the Great American Southwest." He shook his head. "How I wish I could go with you!"

Quatsch! Adler thought, exasperated. This beat-up monkey was leading the organ grinder. Well, best he played along with Ross for now.

"You know the native people?" Adler asked Wheeler. He grinned, showing both gapped and chipped front teeth.

"Married into them, *Herr Doktor*! Had me a fine little Indian wife. Hardworking. Kept me fed."

"Where is she now?"

He scanned his knuckles. "Well, her family went against me, truth to tell. Turned

88

her mind. She threw me out. But I'll get back in her good graces, and then, her peoples.'"

"You are not of them?"

"Me? No, sir. Mestizo's how they put me on the last census. Some Cherokees on my mama's side, along with the Mexican. Papa was white, maybe even from Connecticut Yankee traders, way back."

Was this mongrel fool the best Ross could do for a guide? "Did you learn any of your wife's language?"

"Oh, sure. Lots of bargain-talk, from when I clerked at the trading post. Some words of affection, too, of course, for the benefit of keeping warm on those mountain winter nights. Getting favors, you know how it is."

Adler sighed. "Can you use them to earn the favors again? Please your Navajo wife enough to—"

"Navajo? Not Navajo, no. My Hania, she's Hopi. Their reservation's inside Navajo country. As different as day and night, them two people. The Hopis live in clay village cities and herd cattle, the Navajo live in huts called hogans, and herd sheep. Navajo men whack out silver jewelry, their women, the wool rugs. Hopi women make the pots and kachina dolls for the tourists, you know?"

"I do not. I was among the Choctaw."

"Oklahoma?"

"Yes."

"Well, the Navajo and Hopi, they're different. On their own land, not transplanted, like the five civilized tribes up Oklahoma way, Doc. The Navajo and Hopi tribal councils fight with each other over water rights and land rights. Don't help that the federals are always changing boundaries, leaving Navajos on Hopi land, and Hopis find themselves in Navajo country."

Well. This information was of use at least, Adler thought. "Their language?" he asked. "It is similar?"

The insufferably talkative man's face cracked into a smile before he slapped more dust off his hat. "About as similar as English is to Chinese. That is to say, different ways of speaking altogether."

Enough. Adler turned to Ross. "I have no need for this man."

Ross looked stunned. "But *Herr Doktor Boerman*. He will be useful, surely. As a guide over the landscape."

"I have not only lived in Oklahoma, Dr. Ross. I studied ancient bones found among the Cheyenne."

"Helmut, my friend. You were never in the high desert of Arizona. Not in the San Francisco and Chuska mountains."

The travel writer knew his geography. Adler brought himself up to his full height, and he was taller than both the men before him. "Like our great Commander Rommel, I do not need to know this desert to lead troops there. Will and imagination will be enough."

"I know good hide-outs," Ross's pathetic Winnetou suggested now.

Adler did not want to be burdened with this man. But Toby Wheeler had the shoulders and arms of a blacksmith and was looking to prove himself. Perhaps he should reconsider.

The man's gap-toothed grin widened. "What do you say, boss? We both want to get back into the Land of Enchantment, *ya*? And you might need to lie low, especially if the military is in town at Fort Defiance. You will not be as welcome with that accent these days."

Chapter 8

Swimming Lessons

Kitty and Luke dismounted, giving their horses room to roam in the welcome shade. She was doing so well with Yazhi. The painted horse with a two-color tail enjoyed her company, was patient and forgiving with Kitty's beginner riding skills.

Luke knew this place, surrounded by cottonwoods. It was for ceremony, women's ceremony—a bubbling spring with a wide enough middle to form a pool, deep enough to drown those who could not swim.

His women now insisted that it serve another purpose. Shade and water for their horses, a classroom for him.

Kitty Charante was born on the island of Manhattan. She could swim. They had both been in battle off one of the many New York shorelines. In the ocean, where he still saw the hand of the German agent floating before his face in the water.

This was different. This was a life-giving spring, a sacred spot. He needed this place, his grandmother said. And his mother and sisters knew he would not question Anaba Bowman's wishes.

It was part of his duty as a Marine, too. They should not have even let him in that branch of the service. There was no such thing as a Marine who could not swim. But they were in wartime, and he had what they called "special skills." So, he was given a personal instructor. The woman who'd placed a love spell on him, without even knowing the proper songs.

That spell was working, getting him into the cool spring water, distracted by how beautiful she was, brimming with health, the water making her bathing clothes cling to her curves.

"Head back, Luke."

"What if I am one of those people who do not float?'

"You'll float. I would not have been able to get you aboard that lifeguard boat if you were determined to sink like a stone." She blew out like a mare impatient with her foal, then spoke more softly, "Everything will be all right, darling. I'm here. I'll help you."

There was a slight tremble in her voice. Was she remembering the time they had cheated death, too? Of course she was.

He leaned back in the water.

"Good. Now, a deep breath. That's it. Let the water assist. Water and air. Now, breathe. Relax. Breathe. Feel my hand?"

"How are you doing this? Holding me up?"

She laughed. "I'm not stronger than I look. Trust the water, love.

Marines need to be able to swim. Island to island. All the way to Japan."

He frowned. "They have ships for that."

"Ships sink."

"Well, this is true."

No. Do not go there. The fear. For her brothers, for him. Alone in an ocean. His fears were like the monsters of Dine stories. Large, small. Too many for him to battle all at once.

"Water is powerful," she said, her voice so soft, so small. He opened his eyes to her, standing over him, a halo of sunlight around her curls.

Had he infected this brave woman with his own fear? "Even desert people know this," he sought to reassure her. "During flash flooding, water in the canyons kill."

He could feel her body shake, even through her hold on his back. "Yes, well. If you can swim, you'll have a chance."

She was remembering, he realized. "You did not kill him, Kitty."

Her mouth tightened. "He would have brought you down, even if it cost his own life. I had to make him let go of you. I was just trying, trying..."

"To save me. You did. My family honors you, loves you for it, as useless as I am to them."

There. A small, trembling smile. She was not meant for this work. The work of war. Was anyone?

"You did not kill him," he repeated. "The water did."

She lightened her hold on his back, reduced it to only her fingers. "Better. That's right, Marine," she said in as gruff a tone as he'd heard her manage. "Fighting chance, in the water. That's all you need. Float. Tread water. Survive. Come home to us."

"Kitty." Those beautiful eyes, full of concern. He was not the only one beset by monsters. Well, that was distracting him, at least.

She smiled. "See? You're doing well. And there's enough swimming room in this pond."

"Spring," he corrected her.

"Spring. I love your springs. We'll teach your family here, shall we?" She stepped away from him.

He noticed. And sank.

She waited.

He came up, sputtering. "You let go of me."

"Minutes ago. Good progress, Marine. Come up smiling next time. For extra credit."

"How did you learn this?"

"What?"

"This way of teaching?"

"The dunking until you come up, smiling?"

"Yes. Just so."

"That's how my brothers taught swimming. They were all lifeguards at Coney Island."

"But not you? You were not a lifeguard?"

"They don't allow girls."

"Foolish."

"Yeah. That's what Mickey and Dom thought. Or maybe they wanted to practice with somebody before they got their first classes to teach, you know? Well, they encouraged me." She laughed. "Called me a mermaid in the water."

"Mermaid? What is this?"

"They're sort of sea creatures from stories we heard as kids. Part fish women."

"Ah. Water Being people. Shapeshifters."

"Yeah. Stuck between shifting, I suppose."

He wanted to get lost in her stories, even though it was not the right season for the telling of them. Stories were reserved for winter. But could they not call it something else, like cultural exchange? They could tell each other how the world came to be, then stories of all its living creatures, and how people, his and hers, should behave among each other. Then he wanted to lie with her in the shade, kissing the still sun-kissed parts of her cheeks, neck, arms, and back.

But she was talking about things called strokes and laps now.

***

Babbitt's Trading Post was the same as when Toby Wheeler had left—a stone building with a tin roof, built in the last century, near the road with a dependable water supply. It was a store, post office, art gallery, and meeting place, with corrals and pens in the back, and extra hogans in the back for long-traveling traders who needed to stay the night. Inside, its counters were of rough timber.   None were gathered in the bull-pen, waiting to be served. Fred Graham, the shy, gangly Anglo youth he remembered, had turned into a man Toby realized as he appeared from the storeroom. Fred now seemed more at ease with his height and frame. He reached into the deep pocket of his apron for the grocery receipt and adjusted his rimless spectacles. Yes, he always had weak eyes. But he was now at ease, and as slow-talking as a Navajo. "Don't remember you so partial to canned sauerkraut, Magpie," he observed from his slightly elevated perch behind the counter.

"Don't call me that, Fred."

"People here go by many names. Did you forget in your time away?"

"No. But that name doesn't sound proper serious enough for my boss."

"Heard some news of him. He's rich and traveled out of Mexico. Got his own cabin at the dude hideaway ranch. Dark glasses, doesn't talk, and in a wheelchair? Sick man, maybe, looking for a cure here in the dry heat, healthy air, curing springs?" He reached behind the counter. "Got his big delivery from Sears right here." He placed another find before Toby. "And his groceries." He pulled out a tin can from inside the paper sack. "Your boss the one that likes sauerkraut?"

"Aw, who's the magpie now?"

He received a slack-jawed smile. "Not me. Me, I'm a friend to all. Don't play favorites, don't tell secrets. 'Mani,' that's what the Hopi call me. Leader. I've risen in esteem since last you were clerking beside me, Toby. I'm director of operations here at the post. Important guy. I get good prices for kachinas, rugs, jewelry. I even buy pelts, just to show my goodwill, you know? I'm respectful of them Ute, Papago, Hopi, and the Navajo. Now, I've got to know what's up, to keep my status. There's a nice white valet's jacket in the Sears order. That for you?"

"I—I'm more a chief assistant. To a very important man."

Graham's smile widened. "The president? Is that who's in the wheelchair? Roosevelt hiding behind those glasses? Did he run out of Negroes or Filipinos for when he travels in Indian country?"

There. Yes. Why not embellish this tale? "You'll get nothing out of me, Fred. Loose lips sink ships."

"I knew it! A government man!"

"Up from Mexico is right. And very important."

"Of course. You're working for a diplomat!"

"Loose lips," Toby said again, with his finger beside his nose. Yes, let him spread that word, this man who now has the job that should have been his.

"Fits in," Fred Graham congratulated himself on his deduction skills, "what with all the brass of the Marines and Army here. And all the government workers taking over at Fort Defiance." He smiled broadly. "Bringing us plenty of business. But does this kraut fancier know who he's hired as tour guide of your old stomping grounds?" He moved in closer. "Listen, Toby, I appreciate you sharing the finer points of bookkeeping. And all the reading to me of far-off places and adventure tales. But let's face it, you left here down in reputation, my friend."

Wheeler looked around nervously. But no one had come into the store. "And why is that? Because I obeyed the law?"

"Went too far in that obeying," Fred Graham said mildly. "You turned against people who trusted you."

"She don't speak highly of me, then?"

"Hania don't speak of you at all. But her menfolk do. None of it good." The manager reached over the counter, lifted the brim of Toby's wide hat, nodding.

Toby swatted the hand away. "Maimed me for life, they did!"

"And they got no remorse for it. They went to jail because you squealed on them, Toby. And they know you're back."

"I did not squeal, I tell you!"

The post manager shrugged. "Well, that's the story. When they came to bring Hania's kids to their boarding school, they took her brothers, too. They were jailed half a year for hiding the young ones. Everybody knows the federals found them after Hania trusted you to bring her piki bread up the canyon to their hideout. So, they figured you led them there."

"I didn't! I was in my cups and too loud talking about it, is all. The federals, they overheard me."

"Ah."

"So, I didn't tell them, not outright."

"Ain't me you have to convince of that, my friend."

"Aw, I should have found me a woman without kids, without brothers."

"Some say that's why you told on the hideout—to separate Hania from her kids. Well, that's Anglo thinking, Toby. You should have known better. That's not the way it goes here. Hania, she's got family. Would always be somebody to look after her and them kids you wanted out of the way. When she threw you out, you were well and truly divorced. And out of the tribe, my friend."

Shadows appeared against the screen door of the trading post's entrance.

"Didn't we pull enough of your beard out, Magpie? Have you come back for us to scalp the rest of your ugly face?"

Helmut Adler pulled the gingham curtain aside from the window. He saw only the trail to the small meadow, and children gathering around a chaps clad singing cowboy. He did not like being dependent on this unkempt fool, who even somehow forgot his can of sauerkraut at the trading post. How could he trust any information he'd gathered?

The villa he'd reserved at the ranch resort was built for rich American families. It had a separate entrance and a smaller wing. It was for the family's nursemaid, he supposed. That's where Toby Wheeler stayed, his servant valet, on call for his invalid master. Adler did not like the forced isolation of his disguise. And he liked the man reporting his latest findings before him even less.

He turned back to their conversation,

"Yeah, sure, things are moving along on the reservation, *Herr Doktor*. Bigger group than last, the new recruits."

"Of the army of the United States?"

"Marines."

As Adler thought, the Japanese were cracking every American code. Because they had embedded themselves for years within America, and by way of cultural exchanges. They knew every slang term, every cultural touchstone of jazz, baseball, and American film. They had broken every way Americans tried to hide their communications.

But they had not cracked this new code.

And unlike Hitler, their leader was not enthralled by the American West, by that fraud writer Karl May's tales of Shatterhand and Winnetou. Helmut Adler looked down at his prosthesis. Colin Ross was right about at least one thing. He was now Shatterhand, here where the code talkers' language was. Where new radiomen were being recruited to help the Americans take back those Japanese islands, all the way to Tokyo.

But soon, faithful German allies, the ones who devised the Enigma machine, would help their friends win their part of the war. Because this code was built on humans. And humans, unlike machines, could be turned, cracked, or killed. Even with the inept servant that Colin Ross had provided, he would destroy this American effort. He would rise in the esteem of his own country and its ally. And he would exact his revenge on Luke Kayenta and his woman.

Chapter 9

Teamwork

Staff Sergeant Philip Johnson had status among the Diné since Luke was a child. He'd translated before President Roosevelt, the first one, Theodore, back at the turn of the twentieth century. Sergeant Johnson's father was a peacemaker. He had helped expand Dinètah for the good of the people. Luke was always taught to look upon him with respect. He was now a fellow Marine, and a man of middle years, and stood before Luke and Kitty. The lines between his eyes deepened, showing worry.

"I understand, Mrs. Charante, that you have special clearance to know about the broad outlines of our program. Beyond your work with radio and teletype machines."

"Yes, sir."

"Jack Spenser's word is good enough for me, of course."

Did he sound entirely convinced? Luke did not think so. Still, he continued, "We need to train more Navajo Marines with... special knowledge, if we're to have a chance taking those islands in the Pacific. It is crucial that the Japanese don't know what we're communicating. The first Navajo radiomen platoons are doing well in the field, exceeding expectations." Something flickered in Sergeant Johnson's light eyes. Distracted by how the blue seemed to reflect the sky, Luke could not read what the man's hesitation meant. Then his shoulders eased and he spoke again, "With your help, and recommendations from the schools, we are scouting these next potential classes of intelligent boys, those fluent in both languages. We know they don't fully trust us. But you. They trust you. And their womenfolk seem to trust Mrs. Charante. We're depending on you both."

He was a White man. Of course, he did not like this dependence.

Luke maintained eye contact, even though he was taught that this was very rude. It was not rude to the bilagáana. "We will do our best."

"Good. I'll have Mrs. Charante assigned with you."

They walked out of Sergeant Johnson's office together. Luke wanted to take Kitty's hand.

She brushed her fingers against his. Was she feeling desire for him, too? "The long arm of Jack Spenser's O.S.S. influence strikes again," she observed.

"Yes. Still, Sergeant Johnson seems worried to me."

"About getting more recruits, or about me knowing of the program?"

"Both, I think."

"Well, at least Jack doesn't want to separate a good team."

"Do you think we are that, Kitty? A good team?"

She snorted and shot him one of her bold, sly-eyed gazes, both amusing and embarrassing him.

Luke frowned. "In our work, I mean."

"Sure. And in wartime, we don't have a choice, do we? So. We're partners again."

"That is the good part of all this."

They turned a corner. No one was around them now. She put her arm through his. Her gardenia scent intensified. "All this?" she asked.

It was time. Time to ask her. "Was it something more than Jack Spenser's kind regard and influence that brought you here, Kitty?"

"Besides his bet with me that I'm a country girl at heart and would enjoy the visit with you?" She shrugged those lovely shoulders, covered in a blouse of deep purple, the last color of a Dinétah sunset. Her face displayed no shame. Luke was now convinced she had no more knowledge than he had. This was something they could work at discovering together, then. "Well, one way or the other, we're in the thick of it now, partner," she said, coming closer as they walked, leaning her head against his shoulder, causing his heart to open.

"I am glad you are over your space and height sickness," he told her.

"And I'm glad you can swim."

"Did Jack want you to make sure I could swim?"

"Well, he might have mentioned it."

"When?"

"When I learned the O.S.S. part of my assignment."

"He sent you here, officially, then?"

"He... got involved in my choices. Discouraged me from signing up with the Cadet Nursing Corps. Consider my ready skills in communications, he said. Then he pulled some strings to get me here after my basic training. I thought he was being kind. You know, including time with your family." She looked up at him through the veil of her dark lashes.

Resist her love medicine, Luke told himself. It was very distracting. "A calculated kindness?"

"I think maybe, yes."

"This sounds like Jack Spenser, who does not trust me yet."

"Luke. We're not in a trusting business. We're to be aware at all times. To find people who are not as they seem."

"We are the same. Not as we seem. Full of secrets."

"Yes," she conceded. "That is the hardest part for me."

He stopped. Faced her. "It is?"

"Of course, my darling."

That endearment. How he loved hearing it. He must overcome his own shyness. He must address her with endearments, too. "How do you see it?" he asked.

"Well, we have two jobs now, don't we? The straightforward part: you're training men in a specialty, the Signal Corps. I'm learning my communications job in the Women's Reserve. But first we were O.S.S., and we are that still. It's wartime. We wear a uniform, and underneath it, the uniform of another service."

"The invisible uniform."

"When called upon, yes."

"And this is one of those secret times. To convince these men. More code men. To convince their families to let them go with blessings."

"Exactly."

He smiled. "I like the way you think of us. I will think of it that way, too. My love." He swooped down and kissed her then. Yes. She liked that. She took hold of his face in those strong hands, their nails painted red.

***

"You loved me, once, Han darlin'. Come." Toby Wheeler placed the paper sack on her kitchen table. "Come away. Have a drink with me at the Gopher Hole so we can talk."

She continued folding clothes. "Drinking gives people the courage to act badly."

107

"Since when have you become a philosopher? Women, they think too much." He reached to touch that sweet spot at her hip. It had always worked. But that was years ago. Her eyes warned him. He stepped back and laughed. "Shall I go alone? Maybe find me a young filly to replace you?"

She would have laughed before. Now, she grunted. "If you can find one foolish enough. But all have been warned against you."

"It was a mistake! A slip of the tongue, Hania. I never meant any harm."

"I am glad to hear from you what happened that night long ago. I am sorry my brothers threatened you again. But you must leave now, Toby. Because I began a circle of harm to my family when I chose a foolish husband."

"Who is returned. Changed! With an important job." He shoved the package toward her. "Look what I brought you from the Halls of Montezuma. Gifts from my work with very important people. I learned many things. Things that can bring us happiness. The world is changing, Hania."

"Change does not come here. We will live as we have always lived."

"You know that's not true. Between the droughts and the Navajo, the Conquistadors and the greedy Americans."

"Which of them are you working for now? Get out. Take your gifts. I have asked my brothers to leave you alone. But my sons are taller and stronger than you are now."

Chapter 10

In Service

"You sure you don't want to enlist with us, Kitty?" Mayme Colton asked.

Caught again, reading her housemate's medical textbook.

"Our service needs women with capable hands, big hearts, and strong stomachs to patch up the men of this war," Mayme continued.

"I considered it. But even the accelerated training is thirty months long."

"Judging from the last one, there will be plenty for us to do for years, I think."

"No doubt." Kitty did not like keeping the real reason for her chosen service from the kind-eyed woman. Mayme's devotion towards the student nurses in her charge at Fort Defiance was inspiring.

Kitty closed the book in her lap. "I had my years as a switchboard operator to build on in my present service."

"Oh, of course, that makes sense."

The fort now encircled a community buzzing with war effort business. Kitty was happy to be a part of it, as much as she missed her on-leave time with Luke and his family on the Navajo reservation. Dinétah, she corrected herself. To the Navajo, this was their country, inside the country of the United States.

Luke's sister Chooli, who plied her considerable skills at the telegraph office, was her guide into her new life in communications training, but Kitty envied the lives of her boys, living with their grandmothers on the family land, herding sheep over the summer. Kitty now slept, not in a corner of Taswan's hogan, but in a barracks style. Here, with Mayme and her nurses, with women learning how to put portable radio transmitting and receiving sets together with a speed that astonished her. And with Women's Air Force Service pilots, busy ferrying planes and training the men.

The women working around Kitty came from all over the states. They were of every religion and color, in overalls or crisp white hospital attire, their hair tied back or in cotton snoods, without fuss or make up except the bright Victory Red lipstick that they all favored because Hitler hated the shade.

"We all are discovering our skills here, aren't we?" Mayme continued, drawing Kitty out of her thoughts. "Don't mind my curiosity. I even pester Doc Carmichael."

"Tweed suit? Plaid bow tie at the dance last night?" Kitty tried to remember the man Mayme had pointed out among the dizzying array of male dance partners. As many as she and her fellow war working women were, they were far outnumbered by servicemen. That meant for aching feet and bruised toes after dance nights.

"That's the one," Mayme said as a slight blush rose to her cheeks. "Local veterinarian. I told him he should go into the people doctoring service. He's got the anatomies of animals, big and small, covered. Still time for accelerated med school training. Adding some shot-up and sick soldiers to his roster shouldn't be so hard."

Kitty laughed. "I never thought of it that way."

"And talking to animals makes you less ornery than a people doctor, it seems to me."

"What did he say to that?"

"Nothing. He's a little shy around women. But he laughed."

"You and Dr. Carmichael are in a mutual admiration society, I think."

The nurse colored to the roots of her red hair, now. Another characteristic she shared with the young veterinarian, Kitty remembered now.

"Did he say something about me when you did a dance turn with him, Kitty?"

"Only that you were not only a good dancer, but a fine teacher. He seems to think he's got no grace on the floor."

"That's not true!" Mayme protested, sealing Kitty's first impression. Because for all his shy charm, Doctor Carmichael was indeed, helpless on the dance floor.

"Well," her roommate huffed, "no one could match the moves of you and your Marine."

Kitty sighed. Luke was already "her marine." Hiding her double life in service of both the Woman's Auxiliary and the O.S.S. was going to be child's play next to trying to hide her romance with Luke Kayenta.

Kitty loved both worlds they traveled together in the tumble-down Navajo service truck. Luke served as her translator with the Navajos who did not speak English. She could feel the homesickness of the new Marines as she carried their letters from Babbitt's trading post to their families. Some stared at her clothes, her paler skin with hesitation, suspicion. She tried to gain trust by way of a quick smile and her admiration of their children. What a great place to bring up kids—full of space and sun and animals to care for.

She met with Sophie Denet Bia, herding sheep with her elder sister below the canyon of the ancient cave cities, making fry bread over an open flame. Sophie's fry bread was better, even, than Luke's mother's. Kitty wanted to learn more about that. But Sophie wanted to talk about her animals, so Kitty listened.

The two sisters did not have dogs watching their sheep, but a donkey.

"Those donkeys are good animals," Sophie claimed. "In the morning, they will wait for you in the corral with the sheep. It is nice to have sheep when you are young."

She drew a half circle with her sweeping arm. "We have fourteen acres down here in the canyon. Corn, squash, peaches, and alfalfa. I graduated from Wingate Boarding School in 1934. I work as a hostess and cook in winter. I can talk to people, all kinds of people. I want to be one of the talking Marines. I asked Johnny Manuelito about it. He was in Corporal Kayenta's first class. He's over there now, across the Pacific. Johnny told me that the Marines are not taking women. Then I hear about you. They let you in there. You talk with them, the radiomen."

"I have similar training. Because my job will be in communications, too."

"I want to be a Marine, like you."

"I'm not a Marine, Sophie."

"Johnny said I should try the WAAC, the Women's Auxiliary Army Corps," she pronounced carefully.

Kitty smiled. "That's the branch of the service I'm in."

"And will you help me to join too?"

"Sure. They just opened a recruiting office in Santa Fe."

"I know the way. I will go there. Ask to join."

"But, judging from this frybread, they'll put you to work feeding soldiers."

"You know the way of them." Sophie considered. "Still, that is good work. I like helping crops to grow. I like feeding people."

"I think you are a bridge person, Sophie, like Luke. She nodded toward him as he rubbed the jaw of the delighted donkey.

"*Aoo*. We are paving a path. For our children and grandchildren. Sometimes this comes with a war. Because the men will come home. But we will still be here. That is how I see it."

That night, Kitty dreamt of their children, hers and Luke's. Children with her smile and his strength, who would fit into both worlds. She woke up alone in her barracks bunk, among other women like Sophie Denet Bia, who knew how to shift their dreams.

***

Toby Wheeler grunted. He'd had too much to drink, again. But he didn't want to face the sour-faced German with so little information. That was his trade, information. But it did not get him his Hania back. Neither had his gifts. She must have found another man, the whore. And she was right about one thing—her kids were now old enough to look at him with murder in their eyes. Her brothers had done enough damage. And with a word from her, they

115

would make his face clean of the rest of his beard.

Not that he was so wonderful to look at, bearded or clean-shaven, anymore.

It had not been a good day. And night was falling. Time to return to the rich gringo ranch, that did not have his new *Herr Doktor's* favorite foods on the menu. Time to play his lapdog servant, so Adler would remain a mysterious, invalid figure. And not starve there in his luxury surroundings.

Toby poured the last of his bottle into a glass for his dull informant of the evening. Might as well try a little more conversation.

"These boys, Navajo and Hopi, both. So ready to answer the call. Of course, what is there here for them? Want to break out into the wide world, maybe, like those in the last war."

"Maybe," the bible salesman from Tucson allowed.

Huh. Not great at conversation, for a salesman. Well, if he talked louder, he might widen the cantina's circle. No, not cantina. He was not in Mexico anymore. Taverns, saloons, honky-tonks, here. This was a tavern, the most genteel of the lot. He should mind his manners. Maybe a little play for sympathy?

"I saw friends shot to pieces, gassed, in the last war," he tried a lie.

"Then the Spanish flu took out plenty of those left," someone standing against the wall commented.

Yes. This is what Toby wanted. A little real companionship. Not that self-serving Kraut he worked for. How to draw this man over? "Left a whole nation of womenfolk," he continued the thread. "That's when I courted my Hania, war widow. Now her sons are lining up for the army. Can't keep the new boys down."

A man at a neighboring table shook his head. "And the Marine recruiters are after all the Navajo they can find. The Long Walk. The reservations. I will never understand the Navajo. State of Arizona says they can't even vote. Why are they so eager to fight for the United States?"

The new arrival, the one who was standing apart, now approached the bar. with his beer still full. "It is not about the United States or orders coming out of Washington. This is their home. These are fierce, proud people, you all know that. No one will take the land away from them. Not without a fight. That's what they're defending."

Some nods. "You talk some sense, Doc."

Toby was not drunk enough to miss this opportunity. "Doc? You work with reservation folks and their ailments, sir?"

"Well, the ailments of their sheep, goats, and horses," he said modestly, "and an occasional mule."

At last, Toby Wheeler thought. Someone who might be useful to know. A connector.

Chapter 11

Whirlwinds

The Marines had taken over the guests-only private pool at Wananda Lodge. Mrs. Emma Wolff, manager, was not amused. Kitty could see that. Prejudice was not restricted to the American South. She'd seen plenty of it in the neighborhoods of Manhattan, even the roped-off dance floors of Roseland. But Sergeant Johnson, in his polite way, had convinced Mrs. Emma Wolff and her well-heeled patrons that they were doing their patriotic duty for the war effort.

Luke helped Kitty corral the new recruits at first as they walked through the dude ranch resort, staring, wide-eyed at tennis exhibitions and small children in pressed seersucker play clothes trying their hands at roping plaster calves.

The pool was surrounded by pinon trees. And so, less distracting to Marines learning to survive in water. And to the more well-heeled patrons, giving up a couple hours of their daily pool time.

Luke held the recruits as they floated on their backs. By hand, then by finger, then by watching. Just as Kitty had done with him.

And with even more patience, she noticed. Soon Luke's shoulders relaxed, his arms lost their stiffness. Taswan's idea was working to melt away the last of his terror in the water. Kitty was grateful for his sisters' scheming. She had almost missed his fear. It had made him more human, somehow. He had needed her. He was overcoming his own last physical hurdle in becoming a Marine warrior.

Perhaps they would keep him here, training other desert Navajo marines to swim? That was possible, wasn't it? But there were others who could do that. There were others to take over his language duties now, too. Other code talkers to teach the next class of radiomen.

They would be sending him, soon, she thought, as she buffed her hair dry with the most luxuriously thick towel she'd ever felt. They'd send him overseas. She'd be denied combat duty, but they needed her skills, too. Could she remain with him, even if they would no longer be partners?

She had to stay as close to him as she could, she told herself as he took her duffel bag and slung it behind his grandmother's plaid blanket in that beat-up truck Kitty now considered their canyon chariot.

"That went well, I think," she offered.

"Yes. You are a good teacher."

"Not without you being there in the water with them."

"Proving they might not sink?"

"Exactly. Partner."

He smiled. Yes. Now that smile was a better achievement than a pool full of floating Marines. How she loved being the cause of it.

***

"Halfway up we can see the whirlwinds form."

"Whirlwinds?"

"Dust tornadoes. Doc Carmichael tells me they're fierce this summer. Make both the Navajo and the Hopi nervous. Scaring the horses, both those tame and the mustangs, like that herd down below. Bad signs of coming evil, you see."

Adler scanned the horizon, then the canyon's floor. His man was lording the connections he was making in his old home again. It was a wider world than the narrow confines of the resort.

"Wind is kicking up one there, see, *Herr Docktor*?"

He did. And the horses were indeed, affected, scattering in smaller groups, while keeping each other in sight through the blinding dust. From their godlike distance above, it looked like a crazy choreography. So American. But then, the galloping somehow co-ordinated, formed a discernable figure whirling through the desert floor. A figure he knew well. A swastika.

120

Helmut Adler's breath caught. He was a practical man, a man of science. He looked askance at Himmler and the rest of Hitler's inner circle's obsession with the occult and ancient German mythology. But there it was below them, for a brief moment: the coming of the Third Reich to America. If he could get these people to turn against each other, like these horses, in their fear.

Then, the formation disappeared in the chaos.

"Might have some company from the panther watcher," Tobias Wheeler said.

"Who is that?"

"Oh, he won't come this close to our hide-out up further up in the ghost village, *Herr Doktor*, don't you worry. He's Navajo, and they got all kinds of death taboos, you know?"

Adler was hardly worried. He had proven his own bravery in two wars. He didn't need the assurances of this mongrel American, who escaped his duty and was only interested in his next drink.

Adler cursed being dependent on Tobias Wheeler. But, at least climbing up to ruins, he was free of that wheelchair and the dark, paned spectacles. Here, he was not the helpless rich invalid, paying handsomely, courtesy of the Third Reich, for his privacy at the ridiculous Arizona ranch.

To fit his new persona, he'd endured endless promises of restoration for his health by charlatan doctors, feeling off the rich. Fortunately, his own silly courtship of Wananda's proprietress, Mrs. Wolff, now kept them from his door. There were always foolish, rich Americans, no matter the state of their economy, he supposed. And the signs of the depression, of a country "making do," throughout the 1930s were fading now that the United States had gathered itself together enough to become a war machine. Fortunately, Mrs. Wolff's isolationist tendencies from the same decade were still in evidence, from their little talks around kitchen delicacies she would bring her "Professor Doctor Boerman."

This excursion into the historic desert canyon dwellings reminded him of his time between the wars, studying native peoples' languages, getting ready to defeat the weapon that had defeated him in the forests of Argonne in 1917. He would avenge those who had been obliterated that day.

But the lowest of his soldiers would have been a better comrade than the ones he was forced to spend his days with now.

Well, at least he was out in the air with the remains of older civilizations. Ones he'd learned to respect. They were more advanced people than their primitive descendants. People of innovative, architectural wonders. Descendants of pyramid builders. Ones that had carved swastikas into their sandstone rocks. Representing whirlwinds, he knew. Well, a whirlwind was coming, America. Old Shatterhand was here to see to it.

Wheeler was still talking nonsense about ghosts haunting this cliff city they were approaching on their climb. "From a long time ago," he explained. "Back when the Navajo lost one of their own children. Runaway from a boarding school. In winter. Froze to death in there, hiding out, they think. Thought this was a good place to hide, that boy. Nobody knows, but the Navajo believe the boy's ghost is there, turned into a *Yei*, a vengeful spirit. They call him Frozen Boy." He cocked his head. "You never taught at those boarding schools, did you professor?"

"No."

"Good. Cause that ghost, he'd come for you, sure. Now the alive one, one they called Panther Watcher, he didn't come for a long time, so I didn't think to mention him to you when you asked about anybody and everybody Navajo. Because for over a year this one's been gone, people say. But now they talk about him again. Because he's back, you see. He is looking over at these buildings of the Old Ones again. But they say it's not so much for the panthers anymore, no, sir. And so, his name? The Navajos changed it."

Alder leaned harder on the walking stick. They needed to keep supplying his place among the cliffs for when he needed it, if they found him out, those endless streams of Americans, training for their invasions of

Japan, of Europe. What did he care about the Navajo's tiresome, constant native habit of name changing? His mechanical hand felt too heavy to bear. He tucked it under the strap of his knapsack. A line of sweat trickled down his back. He was thirsty in the rising heat. But he did not call for a stop. Keep up. Don't show this fool guide that he needs rest, Adler thought. Besides, what he really needed was rest from the man's constant babble.

"Love Struck. That's his new name, see? Because they say, while he was away, his heart was captured by a city woman. Those pueblos put her city life in his mind. 'A Mexican woman, maybe?' I ask. No, he did not go South when he and a clan brother went away. Nobody knew why. Big secret. But the clan brother did not return. He did not come back so bad that Love Struck, he needs a ceremony, they say. Because he's so out of *hózhó*, out of balance."

Adler stopped, but not from weariness. His senses ignited. He took Tobias Wheeler by the shoulders.

"Who is this man?" he demanded.

"Easy, *Herr Doktor*. Those pincers of yours hurt! Love Struck Warrior is what I call him now. Because I can play these games with names, too. I even caught sight of him in high moccasins over soldier trousers. Fancy ones, Marine recruiter ones. He was with a woman. A white woman."

Adler stopped. "What white woman?"

"You need to rest, maybe? Our packs are heavy today."

"What white woman?" Adler demanded, louder.

"One who trains with the communications women at Fort Defiance. With the telegraph operator. And bunks with the army nurses. Quite the swimmer. She's the talk of our place, Wananda."

"What are you saying, man?"

"You'd know if you'd let me wheel you out among the swells once in a while, *Herr Doktor*. At the Olympic pool at Wananda, this woman is teaching new Navajo recruits. Because they don't let them in the Marines until they can swim. Sure, ask Miss Emma about them when you're finished talking about how well Germany's rounding up Jews and invading Russia. Miss Emma got strong-armed into it as her patriotic duty now that there's a war on. Now, the swimming instructor, she's a widow from back East, this mermaid of the Marines. My Hania was a widow, too, a war widow. They make good wives. Have had a taste of the carnal delights, are hungry for it, you understand? Well, this one, young Love Struck kisses her like she's his last meal when they are off duty and come up here."

Adler wanted to wipe the self-satisfied look off Tobias Wheeler's face. No wonder the man had his nose broken so many times. No wonder his beard only grew on one side of his face. Someone had ripped half of it out.

Wheeler's grin widened. "There. I thought you would like to know more about them two, since you're so interested in the recruiters."

"His name, man! His actual name!"

"Well, that would take some time," Wheeler said slowly. "See, proper Navajo introductions come with the clans of his people—his mother's, then father's, then the clans of his four grandparents.' They do names up real proper, the Navajo do. But to us folks, he'd be known by his facing-out-to-the-white-world name."

"What is it?"

"Kayenta. Luke Kayenta."

Adler took a deep breath. There would be no more justifying his existence in the Third Reich by counting the numbers of troop car trains heading out of Flagstaff station, no more fruitless searches for angry Japanese civilians to turn into spies. They were alive. And they were here, right here, the French-Canadian pilot's wife and that damned Red Indian.

He had not pulled them down far enough into the depths of the Atlantic.

This bumbling fool had found Luke Kayenta and Kitty Charante.

Well. They would soon become reacquainted.

Chapter 12

Scorpions

Luke screeched the Navajo Service truck to a halt. Slow, now. Calm. That's what his Kitty was, there, beside him—calm and strong, even with the convulsing animal in her arms, the crying child beside her. Follow his woman's example, for all their sake, he told his racing heart.

He read the small, shingled sign hanging outside the door. They had arrived.

Peter Wilson was the first Anglo veterinarian to live in Dinètah. He'd rented a shack that Clarence Gorman had set up as a tourist stop for Mr. Fred Harvey's bus excursions, back when Luke was a child. It was a smart choice. Because Clarence was a Singer, and the veterinarian showed respect to a fellow medicine person. And he was always on time with the rent.

The plank walls of the first room were still decorated with shelves of pots, decorative dolls, and rugs left over from the gift shop. It was his reception area, equipped with mismatched chairs, a desk, and a single file cabinet. No other veterinarian worked respectfully with the Diné. Before Dr.

Wilson, the vets would only fit them in around their White farmer clients.

Luke hoped the man could help.

But there was no one there. Was he out on a call?

A young man entered the room, pushing his spectacles up the bridge of his nose. He was a pale Anglo with flaming red hair. Small in stature, but with the muscled arms of a man who knew his way around a birthing stall.

"Where is Dr. Wilson?" Luke asked, impolitely demanding, because his nephew's tears were soaking his shirt.

"Off to Maine at his sister's lake house. My first summer in charge alone. I'm Evan Carmichael...associate, now partner."

Nastas stepped forward with Kitty, his hand on the swaddling blanket she held around his dog. "Yiska saved us from a whole swarm of scorpions. Can you help him, Doctor?"

"A swarm? Highly unusual." He shifted his gaze to Luke. "Hiding under a rock, were they?"

"A bowl," Luke said.

"Well, we care for large animals mostly, but I'll have a look at such a brave creature." He hesitated. "If the dog's boy will allow it."

His nephew nodded his tear-stained face.

Kitty unwrapped her bundle and held out the dog's paw for the doctor's inspection. "Nasty. And painful. Not usually deadly."

"Even in one so small as Yiska?" The cry cracked through his nephew's voice.

"Even so. Let's see if we can help the poor fellow. Come."

They followed him to the more whitewashed treatment room, full of microscopes, test tubes, and petri dishes.

"He's a good herder," Nastas said, as Kitty released the dog to the table. "He can bring in sheep many times his size."

"Indeed? Is he bred for it? Got some English border collie in him?"

Nastas returned a puzzled look.

Luke was more practiced than his nephew at keeping his face neutral in front of *bilagáana*. "We do not breed dogs, sir," he said. "We train those who enjoy the work and our sheep. They connect."

"And this little guy connects so well, Doctor," Kitty said.

"Well, now. We all need to relieve our fellows of suffering," Doctor Carmichael agreed. He squatted beside Nastas, small for his eight years. Luke's heart clenched. The boy looked smaller, younger, in his distress over his dog. The doctor spoke softly. "You are a good friend of Yiska. You and your parents did the right thing to bring him in."

Nastas provided a shaky smile. "Oh. No, sir. My father works on the railroad. This is my Uncle Luke. He's a Marine. This lady is called Kitty, Mrs. Charante. She can swim, even in the ocean. I am Nastas, this dog Yikas's boy."

"Oh, I beg your pardon," Dr. Carmichael said, his gaze shifting, reevaluating them, Luke thought. "The way you two dance, I assumed you'd been doing it for years. And now I place you. The Marine recruiter and his back-east lady. Well. Very pleased to make formal acquaintance, off the dance floor, with you all."

That settled, the kind-eyed vet went to work, cleaning the wound.

The smell of Fels Naptha laundry soap brought Luke back to his boarding school days when speaking his language would get his tongue a cleaning. He lost his holding-grip on Yiska's paw. But Kitty was there to take over the task while Dr. Carmichael sent Nastas into his ice box for a cold compress.

"What we're doing should ease the pain and reduce the swelling," he said, concentrating on his still shaking, but now silent, wide-eyed patient. "There's calm at the center of your storm," he observed. "You know we're trying to help, don't you, Yiska?"

Luke slipped his arm around Kitty's waist as she maintained her hold on the small paw. Nastas stroked his dog's head and continued encouraging Yiska to be brave and calm.

"There's not a lot we can do," Dr. Carmichael admitted. There is no antivenom for scorpion. And you are right, Nastas. Yiska is a small dog, who has endured three stings, by my count. But a colleague of mine up Cincinnati way has been experimenting with a treatment. He sent me some syrup when I told him about all the creatures that sting and bite down here. We could try it."

"What is this treatment?" Luke asked.

"It's a drug that opposes the activity of histamine receptors in the body. It will not get the venom out, but might help Yiska's small body to fight through its effects."

"To bring himself back in balance?"

"Yes, exactly."

Luke took Nastas' slight shoulders between his hands. He wished Chooli and the women were here. But Kitty was, with her trembling, encouraging smile, and her nod. Luke and the boy came to a silent understanding before he faced the doctor again. "I leave the decision about this treatment to my nephew."

Nastas took hold of his sleeve. "Do you trust Dr. Carmichael, Uncle?" Nastas whispered in Diné.

"*Shidii.*"

"Aunt? What do you think on this?"

Kitty blinked. At the honorific his nephew had bestowed on her, or the question, Luke wondered. "Worth a try, kiddo," she said.

"And the doctor talks like us about animals. Mostly. It is agreed."

The doctor smiled. "Thank you. Thank you for your trust, folks."

Luke was liking the man more and more.

Kitty held Yikas in her lap as the syrup was gently administered. "Your Aunt Kitty has nerves of steel," the doctor observed to Nastas and Luke. "If I had more work, I'd like an assistant of her caliber."

Kitty gave out a small laugh. "No, you wouldn't, Doc. I'm a city girl, still getting used to horses. And I stay clear of goats altogether."

"Look," Nastas summoned them with quiet wonder. "Yiska stops her shaking. She breathes better, too."

"I think you're right," the doctor confirmed. "Well. I look forward to reporting to my Cincinnati colleague about his concoction. Yiska can continue to recover at home or your sheep camp. Keep the wound clean. Keep her quiet. Observe her condition. Oh, and keep your spaces clear of standing water. Draws scorpions."

Luke offered his hand. "Thank you, sir."

"Well. Thanks for visiting me in my loneliness."

"We will send others. Best to keep your hat on in summer on the canyon floor."

Doctor Carmichael scratched his red mane. "I'll do that."

It wasn't until Yiska was bundled next to her boy for the night that Luke drew Kitty from her visit at his mother's hogan. He showed her the bowl that contained the scorpions.

"Kitty, is this yours? Did you buy it at the trading post?"

"No. I've never seen it before."

"Neither have I, nor anyone else."

"It's not one of your mother's or sisters'?"

"See the design?" He turned the small bowl so she could see the inside.

"Yes. Beautiful. It looks like feathers."

"Yes. It is called the four winds. When the artist fired it, she made fire clouds— those dark areas of deep colors. "It is not a Diné-made bowl, Kitty. It is Hopi."

"What does this mean?"

"Someone left it there at our camp, I think."

"Luke, I have never even met a Hopi person. Oh, except for the little family on the train."

"The doctor is right. Scorpions do not gather on their own except in winter when they nest for warmth." Luke considered his words carefully. "And we already know to keep standing water away from our homes, our camps. We live with and respect the scorpion, since before it disturbed the balance of the First World."

"My."

"Trouble has followed us, Kitty. Someone with bad intentions, I think. Our brave Yiska protected us, protected his boy, one who is also small and could have been very hurt."

"Oh, Luke. Nastas said the bowl sat among our jackets, yours and mine. It's why we didn't see it. But Yiska did. This harm. It was meant for us, wasn't it?"

"I think this is possible, yes."

"What should we do?"

Luke held the bowl before her. Their fingers joined around it as he pondered her question. "We can start by finding the one who made the pot, I think," he finally said.

"How?"

He smiled. "Well. You said that you know some Hopi women?"

"Missionaries, traders, surveyors, photographers, and ethnographers, we have grown used to among us." The woman observed mildly. She was about his mother's age, Luke thought, perhaps older. It was hard for him to tell. Women were beautiful at all ages. "But a Diné?" she continued as she scrutinized him slowly, from his feet up to his hair. "And one as tall as a tree? That is a rare honor to my house."

Standing beside him, Kitty looked nervous. There was no time to translate. Luke had to devise an answer to her greeting. One in her own language.

"Women of our own people share a delight in noting my oddness. In that you are one." Luke was not sure his words and observations would be taken well or as an insult. He watched the woman's face.

A grimace.

"Ugh. Drink my tea and stop butchering my language." She nodded politely toward Kitty. "We will speak in English with my daughter's friend."

Kitty nodded, smiling. They were both smiling. United in their delight of his own bumbling efforts, Luke suspected. Kitty looked more at home here in the Third Mesa town of Oraibi, which, except for the altitude, resembled the constructions of her village section on the island of Manhattan.

They continued sipping their host's offering, the mild, slightly sweet tea that all the high desert people made from the hearty Greenthread plant.

When they finished, Kitty unwrapped the bowl from its paper and offered it to Winona Sakeva.

"We are trying to learn where this came from, Mrs. Sakeva," she said.

As she turned it over, Luke watched a slight tremble in the woman's fingers. The humorous lines beside her eyes disappeared.

Finally, she spoke. "It has not been signed. It does not have a broken spirit line, made to sell."

Kitty raised her eyes to Luke's. "The bowl is part of a household's belongings," he answered the question there. "But without a signature, it is hard to find whose household."

"Not so hard, *Siyázhi*," Sakeva corrected him, softening the correction with a Diné endearment for him meaning 'little one.' We Hopituh-nu-mu can tell one of our spun bowls from another. I have two daughters. One you have met. You helped her and her children, on the train, Mrs. Charante. That is

135

why I speak to you. And with your man, who also does things in the right way." She sniffed. "For a person of Dinétah."

Kitty looked to Luke. He tried to make his eyes say wait. Listen.

They did, together.

Once her fingers became calm again, the woman continued, "Both of my daughters make good pottery. This was not made by the daughter you have met. It was made by her older sister, the born-first one, Hania."

"Does Hania live here in Oraibi?"

"Oh, yes. And I already have heard the story of her 'gone missing pot.'"

Luke waited. Was it a long enough time? "We would like to hear it."

"Yes." Kitty said, much more slowly than she usually spoke. "Would you tell us?"

Their host considered for a long time. Kitty made that sound between her lips again, the way the horse who loved her did when out of patience. But softer. Luke was grateful for that.

"It would be better if she told you herself, I think."

Kitty smiled. "Of course. Might we meet with her? And return the bowl to her?"

Mrs. Sakeva's eyes narrowed. "And ask her how it might have come into your hands?"

"That too," Luke admitted.

"You are a good man, Newcomer. And we like your sister, who takes our messages along the wires. Yes. I will allow this. Hania lives nearby. Come with me."

Hania's steeped tea's scent was also very like the tea Luke's women brewed. But she added a whitening trickle from a can of evaporated milk. Such a small amount would not sour in Luke's stomach, Kitty hoped. He tolerated the egg creams she made for him and his family, after all.

But Winona Sakeva, who'd brought them to her daughter's apartment, misread his wince as he looked into his cup. "Not to your liking, Newcomer? His people stole Greenthread from ours," she explained curtly to Kitty.

"*Ingu!* These people are my guests," her daughter admonished.

Winona Sakeva shifted in her chair in the grand, displeased way that Kitty's Great Aunt Valentina did. "It would not be the first time that thieves drink tea here."

Was that remark made to catch Luke off guard, just as he raised the brew to his lips? If so, this small dispute between mother and daughter failed its purpose. It only made him smile in that sweet, unassuming way Kitty loved. Still, it seemed to satisfy their new host, who looked like the woman Kitty had met on the train: small, beautiful. But this sister showed evidence of a more hard life etched on her face as well as grey streaks among her whirled hair strands.

Hania stared at the small pot as she began her story.

"I was married to a good man. He was a warrior for the United States like you, Newcomer. He came home wounded, suffering in his breathing. But a good man, and gentle, with our children. After he died, I took another husband, a clerk at Babbitt's store, who was an outsider, but good to us. For a while. Then, his actions were not so good. He called my brothers "hostiles" and betrayed them. He betrayed my children, who would not cut their hair or go to the Baptist school. I divorced this man many years ago. Now he has returned. Wanting me. Part of him is still there, longing for our past life. But another part of him is like a corpse, I think, in the power of another. That part of him took my pot, I think."

"Is this the one?" Kitty asked softly.

"Yes." She took the coiled clay bowl from Kitty's hands. "It is different now. Filled with evil intent. I think I will break and bury it."

Her mother looked relieved by Hania's decision.

Luke looked to each woman. "Do you need protection from this man?" he asked.

The younger one smiled. "Oh, no. I have my sons and my brothers, Newcomer. Do not add yourself. There is enough trouble between the Hopi and the Diné. I am sorry for your trouble. It will be buried, and the balance between our families restored."

She lifted the top of the woven basket beside her and pulled out a pendant. Into its green surface was carved a hummingbird dancing around a flower. "He brought me this from his time away. I will bury this, along with the pot," she promised.

"Luke," Kitty said as they walked together toward the truck. "They never heard our story. We didn't tell them about the scorpions, about poor Yiska being stung."

"True enough. Not in words. I think the pot and the stone told them, maybe."

"What is going on?"

He shook his head. "We need to know. We need to find this clerk. He has returned from Mexico, I think, from the gift he brought."

"How do you know that?"

"It is made of Mexican jadeite. I have seen others like it when we meet to trade with people who are not Diné. It is in the style of the Aztec people. A hummingbird was carved into it. This man, who was her husband, is courting her again, like the hummingbird courts the flower."

"She never gave us his name. She loves him."

"She did once, I think. And love is powerful. She has chosen not to let her love turn into something ugly because of his betrayal of her brothers and her children. She knows if the actions of this man threaten

139

my family, I will find him. I will kill him, if I must."

"Luke."

"She has given us all she can, Kitty. She honors us with her trust. "We must find this man, find out about this power that has made him dangerous. And why he directs it at us."

***

Toby Wheeler's employer was pleased. "This was the beginning. Just so. They must know I am coming for them."

"But I did not know about the child joining them that day. And the dog. So many scorpions, so small a boy."

Adler only smiled a thin-lipped, steel smile. "Yes. Relatives. Going after their relatives, their animals. I like this idea of yours. It fits our larger purpose."

"What are you talking about?" Toby felt the sweat lining his back. He didn't mean this. He never meant harm, not real harm. He just wanted Hania back. He just wanted a place here. And be a hero in her eyes. To be part of her future. The glorious future that the two German men in Mexico talked about. "We're here to stop the Navajo radio talkers from going to war. That's what you talked to Dr. Ross about. That's what I agreed to help you do."

140

"And you do not understand what war is, great hero of the last one? The one who saw your comrades gassed? Liar."

"That... was a strategy."

"A lie. You are a charlatan, Tobias Wheeler."

"And you are something better, *Herr Docktor*?"

"All spies are liars, of course. But I have better, higher motivation, you see? I tolerate your incompetence. I charm that ridiculous widow. I must save you Americans from yourselves. Bring you into better discipline. Usher in a New Age. We must think wider at this time, Tobias. We must devise a way to start them warring with each other, these Navajo and Hopi. Divide and conquer, you see?"

"Yes, yes, of course." Enough talk of killing, at least, Toby thought. And the personal vendetta Adler seemed to have against Mrs. Charante and her Navajo Marine. Toby had no use for stiff-necked servicemen, dancing with the women, turning their eyes from men like him. "The army recruiters, they are talking with the Hopi. Like the Marines have their hooks in the Navajo young men. Sure, *Herr Docktor*. We can turn them against each other."

"Yes, yes. They are traditional enemies, you said. What do they fight over?"

"Water."

Chapter 13

Water Rights

At first, Luke thought it was a trade meeting. They sprang up spontaneously, sometimes at a crossroads, especially when tourists were more numerous in the area, before the trains got crowded with troop transport. Blankets were rolled out, silver jewelry, baskets, and pots put on display in the shining sunlight. For sale, among the tourists, for barter among themselves and neighboring Hopi and Apache. Sometimes a prized animal was on hand, offered for stud. But here, now, the angry Hopi cattle drivers had no goods, only a parched-looking herd. Lowing with thirst.

Their ride to Babbitt's trading post to find out more about Scorpion Man would have to wait. Something here was very wrong.

Luke knew this place. There should have been water here this time of year. Water from the spring flowed near the foothills of Red Rock Canyon. Instead, angry Hopi herders held his struggling nephews by their arms. Roughly, as if they were thieves.

He and Kitty dismounted.

"Uncle!" Nastas called out to him. "We do not know these ones! They are not from here."

A Hopi boy of about Shadi's ten years stepped forward. "But we know you," he declared. "You are water stealers from Dinétah!"

"We were looking for a stray, Uncle. We did not know we'd crossed over to Hopi land. They took her. They took our lamb—Galbáhí, the one who runs like a cotton-tailed rabbit."

A pitiful bleat sounded from the cornmeal sack the young herders struggled to hold.

"Please stay behind me, Kitty," Luke said in a low, even voice while handing her his horse's reins.

She obeyed, but he felt her weight shift to a warrior's stance.

Luke opened his arms, stretched out his fingers, to show the young cattle herders and the men behind them that he was without malice.

He cleared his throat and tried his best, most respectful Hopi greeting.

It was answered with a torrent of anger.

Kitty took hold of his sleeve.

"Luke's what's going on?"

"I am trying to find out," he told her and continued addressing the Hopi in English. "These boys are my sister's children. They are under my protection," he said calmly.

A herder in a red vest nodded. "You are the warrior who came home without his clan

143

brother. The one looking for others to fight Roosevelt's war. They should stay here; the Diné you want in uniforms. They might need to fight us!"

A grey-haired herder stepped forward, stopping the men's advance. "Let the boys go free. We will talk with their uncle," he said with quiet authority.

The younger cattlemen grumbled but did as they were instructed. Released from their hold, Shadi and Nastas ran and stood like small fellow guardians on either side of Kitty.

The cattleman elder spoke again. "This one." He nodded toward Luke. "He may now wear the soldier's stripes of the White warriors, but he makes good silver. We traded once. An ornament for my wife's hair, my bridle for his pinto. It was a good trade. My wife praised the workmanship. And the fine turquoise."

Luke remembered their barter at the crossroad. "The bridle still sits lightly in beauty on my woman's horse, see it?"

The man approached closer. Nodded at Yazhi, who granted him the space closer to Kitty with a warning huff. "Will you tell me what has happened here, grandfather?" Luke asked.

"Our cattle know this spot. But it is changed today. Water channeled away, over that ridge. Made to flow and pool into Dinètah. We found the pool. And these boys."

"It is where our lamb strayed, I think," Luke observed. "Look at the size, the years on them. These young ones are looking after my mother's sheep. They did not change the course of the water."

"Still, it is water diverted from our land."

Luke surveyed the section of the freshly built channel. "I can help you bring the flow back. My woman will too."

The red-vested cattleman sneered. "A White woman?"

Luke turned his head, stilling him with a pointed stare. "She is stronger than she looks, this one." He stepped to the side, revealing Kitty, her wide stance matching that of her smaller sentinels. "She is a guest of my grandmother, my mother, and my sisters. An honored guest. We call her Yanaha."

The men shrugged. But their elder said, "*Um Waynuma*?" in Kitty's direction.

"Luke?" Kitty whispered from the side of her mouth. "What should I say?"

"*Ahéé*," will do, Kitty."

"*Ahéé*," she repeated.

The leader smiled. "Give the boys their lamb."

He faced an objection. "Grandfather, how will they pay us for what our cattle have endured?"

"The young ones are not at fault. Neither is this one and his warrior woman, who will help us bring the water back."

"And will they find which of the Diné had caused this trouble?"

"The lamb," the elder said again.

The sack was opened, and soon a struggling Galbáhí found her footing and jumped into the arms of her boys.

Luke looked towards where the sun was in the sky. "Can you return Galbáhí and the herd home?" he asked Chooli's sons.

Shadi nodded. "We can, Uncle."

"But what will happen?" Nastas asked. "Will the cattleman try to drown you?"

Luke smiled. "With our Kitty to protect me? They will not stand a chance."

"Still," his older brother considered. "Will you need our baseball gloves? They have great value."

"No. Tell the women we will be back soon."

"You are sure of this, Uncle?"

"Yes."

Shadi put his arm around his smaller brother as they turned. The lamb followed, hopping, happily nudging Nastas' shoulder.

Kitty faced Luke. "The boys are worried. What is going on?"

"Shovel diplomacy. Can you dig?"

"Sure."

"Good. Someone has ripped up the landscape. We need to help these people."

"All right then," she said uneasily.

"That's my Yanaha."

"You told them the name you gave me. My sacred name. I thought it was something you did not tell everybody."

"This is true. Names have power. To use, when necessary."

"And it was necessary?"

"Yes. Part of the diplomacy." He held out his hand for hers. "Come. These Hopi cattlemen wait for us. With their shovels. They will evaluate our usefulness. And have more demands, maybe. We are the boys' ransom."

"Oh. Well. How exciting."

As they walked to higher ground, the workers already digging to restore the river's flow grumbled, but gave them a wide berth. Luke spoke quietly. "This land is called Moencopi. It is part of the Hopi reservation inside the Navajo lands."

"Inside? How did that happen?" Kitty asked.

"Well, there was so much hostility between the Navajo and Hopi that a part of Navajo land was carved out for the Hopi back in 1891. Boundaries moved a couple more times since. Add to this mess the fact that the Hopis raise cattle and the Navajo sheep."

"But I thought the Hopi live in apartments, up there. Like Mrs. Sakeva and her daughter."

Luke pointed with his chin above them. "Yes, the Hopi are pueblo people, in villages on top of the mesas. But they graze their animals down below here in summer."

"Unless someone diverts the water?"

"Yes. These herders think we Diné people have done this, trying to drive their cattle out."

"Do you think so?"

"It is possible. But I know our Diné neighbors. What is done here would benefit none of them," he said it, both for her as she climbed down into the channel with him, and for the Hopi men there, who handed them shovels.

Luke felt along the still-damp ground, then pushed his hat back. It was as he suspected. "This diverting channel was done in haste, and badly, but by people who know our close boundaries. Done to stir up bad feelings between us, I think."

"By whom?" the influential elder, who now stood above them, demanded.

"I do not know," Luke admitted.

"Why?"

"I will try to learn both these things, grandfather."

"Good," he said. "No more ransom today. We will all go home now, Newcomer. Tomorrow. More digging. And answers."

"Wow." Kitty wiped a streak of dirt from Luke's brow. "Are we in the middle of a Western movie like *The Cheyenne Tornado*?"

He grunted, helping her up to the parched surface. "It does not feel so exciting."

"What? You don't have a pearl-handled pistol to avenge the murder of Lafe McKee after exposing a crooked poker game and becoming the hired hand of a blonde temptress?"

"I have a shovel only. And home before dark with my raven-haired temptress is the best I can manage."

"With both of us covered in mud?" she finished for him.

He took her grimy, offered hand. "Kitty. We cannot undo this alone."

"Oh, my. We *are* in a western movie. Send for the cavalry!"

He winced. "Call them... reinforcements."

"Oh." Nervous laughter bubbled up from her throat. "Of course."

They walked toward their horses. "Our Marine swimmers are doing well, Kitty?"

She smiled. "Very well. But I'm sure they would welcome an excursion under these beautiful desert skies. Even ditch duty."

He frowned. "Peacekeeping. We will call it peacekeeping when we ask for their help."

"Good idea. But they are very fond of their corporal. They will follow him anywhere."

He grunted. "As long as his woman is beside him, I think."

"In water, mud, or sand, she will be. Sir." She saluted smartly.

Chapter 14

Ditch Duty

"Kayenta!" Get out of there!" Marine Major Gilford shouted.

Luke shielded his eyes to look up at his superior. There were not bars but a rising eagle on the uniform of the grim-faced army officer beside him. That man's ire was directed at his co-commander, the private first class beside Luke. "Conway! What in blazes are you doing?"

Conway's at-attention stance eased into a slouch. "I come from a family of ditch diggers, Colonel, sir. Didn't we channel our way off the Hudson River into a thousand canals long, long ago in the last century?" he said cheerfully. "And didn't we offer some guidance to Corporal Kayenta and his crew, my men and I?"

"We're all off duty, aren't we then, sirs?" the man beside him volunteered. "Is helping keep peace amongst the locals not allowed then?"

Rising Eagle man was not amused. "You're still a part of this man's army, Private!"

"Oh, aye. And aren't our blistered marching feet aware of that?"

"Damned Irish," he muttered as he looked into the sky.

Then the colonel noticed Kitty, Mayme Colton, and her squad, approaching from the Navajo Service truck, laden with sandwiches and a thermos of coffee. "What? Kayenta's enlisted the nursing cadets as well?"

"And didn't Napoleon say that the army marches on its stomach, sir?" the private asked cheerfully.

"I think it was Frederick the Great, Flynn," Conway countered.

"Aye sure, they were both great, sir. But Napoleon got Josephine to boil up some soup in glass jars for his men, did he not, now?"

"Would someone explain to me what's going on?" Major Gifford demanded.

Private Conway smiled. "Local goodwill with the locals, sir. Plain as that. Helping to get the animals watered and the peace kept. Corporal Kayenta will provide the details."

"If you and your Irish brigands will let him get in a word edgewise."

"Just so, sir. But his folks don't believe in interrupting. Real polite, the Navajo are." He caught sight of the women and their sandwiches and nodded to them cheerfully. "Not like us New Yawkers, eh, Kitty?"

Private Flynn shoved Luke forward. "Go ahead, Chief. Tell our beloved commanders how we're preserving the peace among your folks and the Hopis, and saving the war effort for the Japs and Jerrys, right? And are we not downright inspired by Corporal Kayenta's words to us, sirs?" he included as an aside to the officers.

Their Marine commander sighed hard. "God protect us from citizen soldiers."

"Amen to that," his Army counterpart agreed.

***

Helmut Adler adjusted his dark glasses around his eyes. He now rather enjoyed this part of his persona. Because he was sitting in a wheelchair, the affluent tourists at the resort thought him a cripple. Perhaps the spectacles had them thinking him blind as well, because they gave themselves and their children an even wider berth. He should have done this earlier; come outside, instead of secluding himself, drawing up lists and plans. He would not have missed seeing his enemies within sight, teaching their soldiers to swim at the pool.

They no longer came, able to identify him, as he had them busy trying to untangle the mischief he and his associate had provided. Mischief that had Mrs. Wolf in a frenzy of fear that the savages would surely raid her paradise here at Wananda, now that

153

they knew its site plan from their swimming lessons.

The woman was growing tedious. It was good that her visits to his villa for their little chats were less frequent. Out on the property, there was plenty of room to speak freely with Wheeler, dressed in his white valet uniform coat, without any of his fellow tourists hearing them. The mongrel's beard was now closely shaved so that his face no longer stood out in its peculiar growth pattern. Adler had insisted on it when he saw stares linger.

"Well, what news, Tobias? Have they gone into battle over the stolen water?"

"Well, no. Not with the White soldiers meddling, along with the Navajo, to return the water to Hopi land."

"Already this has been done?"

"Listen, I'm as surprised as you are."

"Incompetence! You said it would be enough. You said the Navajo and Hopi were already at war."

"They have been, for centuries. Even in this new overseas war, the recruiters knew enough to keep them separate—Marines came for the Navajo, the U. S. Army for the Hopi."

"So, the Axis powers, a common enemy, have united them?"

"That, sure. And this peacekeeper enemy of yours, *Herr Docktor*."

"Peacekeeper?" That was not Kayenta's reputation in the Spanish prison he burned to the ground, or the five of the best Abwehr agents he killed in New York. Adler fisted his good hand. "They think they have finished with me, Kayenta and his woman. I intend to keep that advantage as long as I can. They cannot trace any of our actions to us?" he asked.

"No, sir. I know how to cover my tracks."

"But they will know. I wish them to know. The ones you hired to reroute the water supply. Can they be depended on to keep quiet?"

"No need. Most have already taken their pay and headed back across the Mexican border."

"Ah, you Mexicans and your guerrilla skills, but your lack of discipline. At one time, you could have gotten Texas and Arizona back, had you but sided with us in the last war."

"That was a long time ago. We're both finding out that everything is changing, not just the relations between the Navajo and Hopi. Now Mexicans are making what the Americans need to fight you. They have jobs in war plants. It was not easy for me to find a few renegades willing to come north to do our bidding. But don't worry, they were barely noticed. And they do not have stellar reputations to make them stand apart."

"And you knew where to find them. Which does not speak highly of your reputation."

"I am an errand boy of Nazis, *Herr Doktor*. That does not put me in exalted company on either side of the border."

"Money, not heritage, puts everyone in the upper echelons of American society, Tobias. Hitler is a great admirer of your industrialist Henry Ford, did you know that? I can see them becoming great friends. Perhaps taking their leisure together here at Wananda, after the war. Hosted by the gracious Mrs. Wolff in a perfect, ordered world like this one, where the rich of the Master Race play at Cowboy and Indian."

"I suppose." Tobias shrugged. "But for now, this whole country's at war. Almost every family is serving the effort, in one way or another, rich and poor. It may not be so easy to turn folks against each other. Even here in Indian country."

"Well. I know how to further stoke their fear of each other. And their vengeance."

"What are you saying?"

"I have a new list for you, Tobias. Of items to order from Babbitt's Trading Post. Scorpions are unreliable. Science is not."

Chapter 15

At the Begay Orchard

Luke's superiors were taking out their hostility toward each other on him, it seemed to him. No more pulling already undisciplined troops into working with the Hopi "locals" on ditch digging. No leave for personal matters, like finding out more about the man threatening his family with scorpions.

Back to basics, his superiors demanded. Back living in the barracks at Fort Defiance. Back in his fancy, uncomfortable Marine uniform. And the worst of it, his partnership with Kitty, dissolved. Luke felt off balance, struggling in high water, without her by his side.

Sergeant Johnson, like Luke, was not a career military man. "We called you in because we're baffled," he explained. "We don't know what's happened to our program. Recruitment has dried up. At first, they said there were vague emergencies at home. Then, they did not return. I thought we had them engaged. I thought they were excited about our project."

"I did too, sir. It must be serious, whatever is keeping them away."

"We thought perhaps you could check on them, their families."

"Perhaps? Perhaps?" his superior demanded. That is not how an order is given! Especially to one of these! Straighten the collar of that uniform, Kayenta! And fill up the next class of those mumbo jumbo talkers!"

And so, Luke's current mission was tracking down reluctant recruits.

His first stop was the Begay Orchard. The heavy air of sickness hung over its grazing land. The family's two brothers were missing from their first interview at Marine headquarters. Luke could see why. The place was in disarray.

The Begay brothers, Billy and Leonard, Luke had known since their days at the boarding school together. Both had expressed interest in the program. They had mentioned clan brothers close by who also had missed appointments at the fort. Now the brothers were at least talking to him as they watched over their sheep.

"These are hard times," Billy began.

"*Shił t'áá'áko*," Luke agreed.

"We do not have your skill at the smithing, Luke. And your family is rich in rug makers."

"Do you not want to be warriors for the Marines?"

Leonard snorted, then called out an instruction to one of their dogs.

"We did," Billy continued. "Until our sheep started getting sick."

"Sick?"

"Bad water. We lost two already. The Hopi. They will drive us out, maybe. If we go into service, they will poison the rest, drive our families off. It is not only us."

"Please. Tell me more of this."

Leonard spoke now. "Our medicine people smell something evil. Some think maybe it comes from the federals and their war."

"The war has thrown us out of balance." Luke politely kept his sights on the sheep and the clever dogs who moved them along as he said, "Japan attacked us. Their forces seek mastery from the west. From the east, Hitler comes to hurt or drive off people who do not look like him."

Billy Begay grunted. "There are oceans each would have to cross."

Luke nodded. "This is true. But there was also an ocean between us and the Conquistadors. Still, they came. Now, the ships of our enemies are better. And they can fly."

"That has been the way of people who came here," Billy conceded.

"And they steal our gold," Leonard said.

"We do not have gold," his brother countered.

"Not yet."

His elder brother rolled his eyes.

"We have coal," Leonard tried.

"A little coal. Mostly rocks and sand."

"Well, I mean the gold of our lives, our ways," Leonard changed tack now.

"Hear me," Luke tried. "We can help the *bilagáana* win back the country of the United States. We can live in peace, not fear."

"Are you sure it is not a Hopi trick, this sickness in our herd? Not a war started because they thought we had taken their water away?"

"We will know soon," Luke promised. "If we call both people together. Here. I will ask my sister Chooli to stand between us as our peace chief. I will ask Doctor Carmichael to look at the sick sheep. Will you help me? Will you provide neutral ground?"

Chapter 16

War Conference

Luke watched the crowd that had gathered around the dead animals of the Begay brothers' herd. Other herders, all of whose sons had been recruited as code talkers, had come, too. Chooli's presence was barely containing the anger.

A Hopi man folded his arms. "We do not poison. Why not check your dead sheep's piss? Maybe it is filled with evil after you stole our water?"

Choolie held up her arms. "This is not helping." Even his sister, a good bridge person and peacekeeper, was running out of patience.

"You Diné started this bad feeling between us," the Hopi man claimed.

Billy Begay folded his arms. "The canals, the water diversion, they were not our doing."

"So, you said."

Luke unbuttoned the blue coat and took it off as he walked from the gathering. Then he grabbed his high moccasins from behind and sat on the truck's fender, putting them on.

161

A sturdy 1937 Buick pulled up beside him. Dr. Carmichael came out of one side, Kitty and Dr. Wilson the other.

As the two vets reached into the back for their big black bags, Luke swooped down on Kitty's mouth with a welcoming kiss.

After, she laughed as she swiped his mouth of the red remnants of her lipstick. "Didn't take long for you to go renegade from your new orders, Captain."

"I am so glad you are here. Did you get to Babbitt's Store?"

"It's where I met the docs having their reunion. I went AWOL myself when they asked me to come on this call."

"We are both renegade, then?"

"It's what we do best, partner. The Marines can bring it up with the O.S.S."

"Well, I appreciate all your company," Dr. Carmichael inserted himself into their conversation, pulling down the wide-brimmed straw Stetson, a newer version of his mentor's headgear. "I'm afraid my Diné is strictly of the Trading Post variety."

"Knowing that your patients came from families with our missing volunteers explains much," Luke told both doctors as they shook hands. "They are here, arguing. Along with their stricken animals. Thank you, Dr. Wilson, for shortening your summer with your sister."

"I've had enough cold plunges in the lakes of Maine. I missed our skies," the older man assured him. "And I missed feeling useful." He frowned. "I might regret that part."

Luke let out a long breath he did not realize he'd been holding. The stench of death reminded him of that earlier time, as a boy, when the federal men came and thinned his mother's and grandmother's herd, shoving their sheep and goats into a ditch, lighting the ditch on fire.

The affable older veterinarian took his shoulder and squeezed. "Let's see what's going on to both men and beasts, eh, Luke?"

Doctor Carmichael had not yet been fully trusted by either the Diné or the Hopi. Some did not even consult with Doctor Wilson, who had become a friend to many families of both peoples. But even the lack of trust was overcome here at the stricken place.

As they entered the fray, Chooli struggled to contain the mix of languages in the raised voices.

"Luke, what are they saying?" Kitty asked.

"There's something wrong with the water."

"What? Is it drying up again?"

"No. It is no good for drinking, cattle or people."

"Whose land is this? Which farmer?" she asked

"There is no private ownership, love."

The doctors tried to converse with the English speakers. A few among the families were talking to them, but most stood away, casting suspicious glances. Finally, two men created a path to the dead sheep. The doctors went to work.

Chooli leaned down and made her request at Kitty's ear. After a curt nod, Kitty called a halt to all side talk with her shrill whistle. Then Chooli nodded solemnly to Teddy Claw, who stepped forward.

"I think the *nááts 'ó' ootdisli* killed these sheep," Teddy confided in a voice laced with fear.

Doctor Carmichael looked to Luke.

"Whirlwind," Luke translated.

"When did it strike?" Chooli asked.

Teddy, who spoke English well, slipped back into Diné. Was it his fear making him do that? Or something else? Luke listened closely, then translated for Kitty and the doctors. "Yesterday. Evening time. Frozen Boy is making the whirlwinds up at the cliff dwellers' place, they say. Hurling them down upon us. He is angry about something, maybe."

Chooli turned to the herder. "What is the reason for his anger?"

"Nobody knows, so far." The man cast a sideways glance at what was left of Luke's uniform. "Maybe he don't like our boys taken away again."

One of the boys, now a Marine, was Teddy's son Jack, Luke knew. "Frozen Boy did not come home," Jack's father continued. "Like another of ours who went away with this one and did not return. What

164

do you say about what is killing our animals, Luke Kayenta?" Teddy asked, challenge in his tone.

Luke faced the father of a boy in the first Code Talker class, who had already been sent overseas, as he and his clan brother Nantai had been last year. Where Nantai still remained, next to a Spanish Crusader in a Spanish tomb.

"The doctors might have a different idea about the cause of these deaths," Luke said quietly.

Dr. Wilson raised his head from a dead sheep's side. "I'll have to check a blood sample back at my lab. But, Luke, I think we may have a biblical plague on our hands."

"A plague?"

"Anthrax," he whispered. "We need to get a vaccine to these animals. The way it's spreading...it almost reminds me of, but it couldn't be. Not here. I mean, even if it could be, why here? It is so remote from the battles, what would be the purpose, the gain?"

Luke came closer, despite the anger of his neighbors, despite the stench of death. Because Kitty walked beside him. "Please, doctor. Go more slowly. What are you thinking?"

"Well, back in the last war, I was stationed in a hill town in France, taking care of army horses. The shepherds of our surrounding mountains, they tried to drive us out, before we saw any battles. Why were our horses well, and their sheep were dying in droves, they demanded. It seems German agents were sent in ahead of our arrival, with germ warfare—anthrax, smuggled into animal feed, killing their sheep, turning them against us, because our horses were well. They'd been vaccinated, you see, before being put into service. But is this happening here? Now? The Geneva Protocol of 1925 prohibited biological warfare."

Luke sighed hard. "I do not think the Axis powers are paying much mind to protocols of the last, or any other war, doctor."

Billy and Leonard Begay, the hosts of their gathering, now flanked Luke, Kitty, and the vets.

Billy said, "We have to protect our herds, my brother. We cannot go off to war when there is war brewing here."

"We can correct this, together," Dr. Carmichael said quietly. It eased the still stricken look of his mentor.

"How?" Billy asked them both.

Dr. Wilson's voice left the battlefields of the last war, and his voice returned to its more familiar, comforting tone. "Taking water samples. Testing for what is wrong."

One of the Hopi leaders stepped forward. "What is wrong is the Navajo do not belong here."

"We are in the most fraught part of disputed land," Luke countered. "It is as if some force knew exactly where to start trouble."

His sister Chooli stood beside him. "A force with so precise a target usually is human."

Doctor Wilson faced her with a grim look. "I agree."

Chapter 17

Deliveries

The long-distance line crackled.

"Can you help?" Kitty asked Jack Spenser.

"I'll send the vaccine down to you on the next flight I can get out."

"Flight?"

"Of course. The WASPS are flying regularly into Winslow airfield. I'll wire you what time to expect delivery. Put the doctors on the line. And Kitty, you were right to contact me. Whatever the source, we've got to build up goodwill with these people fast."

"But why here, Jack? Why not infect the food supply of a city, or an army base?"

Luke looked to Kitty. He found the same dawning understanding of possibility. Someone was infecting sheep. And trying to kill the code talker program.

His hand bridged to Dr. Carmichael's shoulder as he addressed both veterinarians. "Tell Mr. Spenser what you need."

She was shorter, even, than Kitty. Luke wondered if her height reached five feet. Slight and steady, like river grass reeds. And

168

she was brimming with health and energy. The afternoon wind picked up her black silk scarf and made it dance around her shoulder. Her coveralls were the deep blue of the evening sky. She reminded Luke of Isabelle Marius, the member of the French resistance he admired. He sent out a prayer for that woman's continued good health.

"I have got an urgent package. Any of you folks speak English?"

Her own English was of the American South, slow like that of the Diné, but smooth and honey-soaked. Luke stepped forward. "We do. And we are the ones in urgent need."

"Captain Kayenta?"

"Corporal here, but yes, Ma'am."

"Jack Spenser described you perfectly. Sends his regards to you and your lady. This is Mrs. Charante, I'll just bet."

Kitty smiled. "Just Kitty, please. And we're so pleased to meet you—?"

"Mildred. Mildred Hemmons Carter, Ma'am, of the Montgomery Alabama Civil Air Patrol Squadron, recently rejected as a Woman's Air Force Service Pilot, as not eligible because of my race. But I met Mrs. Roosevelt when she visited Tuskegee, when I graduated. She was so gracious, I was tongue-tied, if you can possibly imagine! Well, she introduced me to your Mr. Spenser, who calls on my abilities from time to time. The O.S.S. has its nose in everybody's hut," the aviatrix confided with a slow wink.

Luke sighed. "That has been the way of it for us."

"You've come with a life-saving package, we hope?" Doctor Carmichael asked.

Pilot Carter re-directed her attention. "The estimable wonders with both small dogs and large animal medicine? Doctors Wilson and Carmichael, are you?"

They both grinned, Dr. Wilson wide, and Dr. Carmichael bashfully. "The very same," he assured her.

"Well now, doctors, kindly tell me what I'm carrying in my humble Piper J-3? A life-saving package?"

"Indeed," Dr. Wilson said. "A vaccine."

"Wait till I tell my mama! She was postmaster of Benson, Alabama. Serving the people of all colors. We both just adore missions of mercy!"

Doctor Carmichael laughed. "The sheep bestow their gratitude."

She snorted. "Wish they'd bestow a mohair sweater." She waved her thumb beyond her shoulder. "Gets pretty cool eight-thousand feet in that tin can."

A bald head appeared in the plane's doorway. "Make that two mohair sweaters." The head acquired a body, and its small frame descended and stood on solid ground with a jaunty dance step.

Bly Kayenta stepped forward in the stunned silence. "You honor us and our home, Sergeant Morgenstern," she said.

The lines beside Isaiah Morgenstern's eyes crinkled deeper in the perpetual amusement that Luke remembered from their days as cellmates in a Spanish hellhole. "So formal, lady!" he objected with a laugh. "But how do you know me?"

"Luke keeps your photograph in an honored spot in my home. And you are always the hero of his stories. His trickster friend of Orchard Street, on the Island of Manhattan."

Isaiah Morgenstern bowed. Then he cast his glance over the entire welcoming party. "But this bunkie of mine, he spoke of only two beautiful sisters. Why did he not mention a third, and the queen of them?"

"I am his mother, sir."

"*Farvundert!* I stand before you, astonished, Madame!"

Luke waited for his mother's eyes to turn sly. They did not. They widened, before she shook her head in amusement.

Behind them, his grandmother spoke. "Come. Try my mutton stew, Stellar Jay and my grandson's Kokopelli," she bestowed a new name on the beautiful aviatrix, and an old one on Isaiah Morgenstern.

Luke and his grandmother put out water for the wild horses, tracing their arrow hoofprints. They were lean, small herds who had been foraging since early spring from plants as wild as they sprouted on the mesa.

His grandmother smiled, with her whole face.

"Your woman has taken to the horses."

"Better than I have to the swimming."

"Keep working at it. We were all born out of water from our mothers. You were still in your sac. I know. Maybe, you were in there, scribbling their *bilagáana* Jesus stories, like who they named you for. You did not notice you were released from my daughter's body. You were not yet finished with your book, huh?"

Luke smiled. "I do not remember, grandmother."

She patted his arm. "Do not worry. I remember for you."

"Thanks."

"Huh. Good thing I sharpened my fingernail, you might be in there still. We have tough sacs, all of this family's women."

"I thank you for my release."

"Ho! You did not thank me then. What a howling out of you, little fish! You wanted to stay inside? You still go inside too much now, I think."

Luke's senses heightened. The air gave him the soft feel of the white wool of his grandmother's *tsiiyéél* bun tie, the texture of the stiff grass bundle his mother had used to comb hair for her that morning. Even the scent of yucca root from the last time they'd washed, it came to him. He became lost in the strands of Anaba Bowman's hair. Then he suddenly felt he would remember this conversation for the rest of his life. That way, if he told it to his children, perhaps the story of his birth would make his grandmother, who had been on the Long Walk, live into the next century.

Her face gifted him with one of those transformational smiles, as if she'd heard his thought. "Some say you are not able to drown, Adits'ah, because of the way you were born. But you do try your gift's patience, getting yourself plunged into both sides of *tónteel*. What is the English?"

"The ocean. The Atlantic Ocean."

"Just so. A bird got you out of the wide water once?"

"A seaplane, yes."

"Then, on the other side, a woman. That woman," she pointed her chin towards Kitty, down by the corral, who was rubbing Yazhi, the horse who had become hers, behind the ears. "Another *tónteel*, big water, wants you swallowed next. Did you know?"

"I did not."

"Huh. Better bring her with you."

173

Chapter 18

Change in Plans

Kitty noticed that the trading post's proprietor, Fred Graham, was as eager to talk to them about Hania's second husband as Hania herself was reluctant.

He leaned over a rough wooden counter of the store. "We both started out sweeping the floors. But Tobias—Toby Wheeler, he was more quick-witted and good with numbers than I was. He taught me how to keep the books, how to get along with every mother's son and daughter who comes through the door. To trade in gossip, information. That's how he got the name, from the Hopi and Navajo folks both— Magpie. But Magpie was too fond of the drink. And he wanted too much of Hania."

"Too much?" Luke encouraged him to detail.

"You don't come between a mother and her children. Am I right, Mrs. Charante?"

Kitty nodded. "Not and live to tell the tale."

The storekeeper laughed. "Exactly! That's been my experience. Don't care where you're from, what color you are, or which set of gods you pray to. Well, Toby sold them kids of Hannia's out to the boarding school, along with her brothers, who tried to hide them up in the canyons. Supposedly, by mistake when he was drunk, as he says, or purposefully. Don't know which. But to the same effect. Too bad. He had a future here. Instead, Hania threw him over, her brothers pulled half his beard and hair out, and our Magpie flew down to his relatives in Mexico. For many years."

"What brought him back?" Luke asked.

"For once, Magpie is mysterious about that. But he works for a rich cripple in a mechanical chair, who Toby calls "the professor." A recent arrival who came to restore his health at Wananda. They say this fellow only talks to Toby and Mrs. Wolff, who owns the place."

Suddenly, the Trading Post's scents of wool blankets, well-oiled machinery, and animal feed intensified. Kitty's senses ignited. "Wananda?"

"Yes, Ma'am. The dude ranch north of here."

She and Luke exchanged glances. "We know the place. And Mrs. Wolff."

"Toby comes in from there to collect packages, to order things for the boss. Always addressed to him, not his professor. From the Sears catalogue, mostly. Don't talk about it. He's gotten much better at keeping secrets, except for, I don't know, an air of importance he carries, you know?"

"Importance?"

"Yeah. Maybe his professor is rubbing off on him. It's like Toby's not just a rich man's servant. His work's going to be good for achieving peace and prosperity, says he. I thought that's what we were all doing, you know? Making our sacrifices for the war effort? But he and his professor are going to end the war single-handedly, it seems! Well, three-handed, on account of the professor lost a hand in the war already. Toby let that slip. That his professor has a mechanical hand."

Luke and Kitty shared glances. Their mutual disbelief vanished in what they saw in each other's eyes, she realized.

"Toby Wheeler. Does he come in regularly?" Luke asked.

"You mean like on a day of the week? An hour of the day?"

"Yes."

"Well, no. Not unless you count the professor's regular craving for sauerkraut. Don't that beat all? A rich man who can have all the fancy food offered at that dude ranch, who favors a can of sauerkraut?"

Luke reached for Kitty's hand as they walked to the truck.

"Luke. How can this be?"

"Hania. Her bowl. The scorpions. The water. The anthrax. Wananda. All of it links to us, there, helping the Marines to swim."

"Luke, do you think Helmut Alder is alive?"

"His body never washed to the shore. The U-Boat was close by. He has found us, Kitty. Somehow, I think he has found us."

"What should we do?"

He closed his eyes. When they opened, he took her hand in both of his. "Kitty. Go to my mother. My sisters. The children. Tell them. Tell Isaiah, their Kokopelli to get word to Mr. Spenser. Chooli will help him. Then be on guard. If Adler has found us, he has found them. I will head for Wananda."

"Luke. Don't go alone."

"Shall I ask for the company of our reinforcements?"

She smiled, finally ready to release him in the care of their Irish canal men allies. "Good idea."

"We must find this man, this Magpie. He will lead us to our enemy."

"I told them our guests are here to enjoy their stay in complete privacy, of course, Mr. Wheeler! Please tell Professor Boerman—"

Adler wheeled himself into the room. "You may tell him yourself, dear Madame."

"Oh. Oh, professor! My sincere apologies!"

"Kindly tell me what has happened here?"

"Well, the swimming instructor, Corporal Kayenta, we knew him, you see, from his time here, with that New York woman, and the way they took over our pool. We had to accommodate the servicemen, of course. I agreed before learning what race the Marines were! I explained we don't admit any of their race here at Wananda, of course. But, but, but... there's a war on, and we must make exceptions. Or so they keep telling me. Oh, the very atmosphere is so very different since we've engaged in hostilities! I thought buying Liberty bonds was quite enough until the ghastly war is over and we can all be friends again."

"Of course, of course. So, these Marines made war on my rooms, then?"

"No, the Army! We never thought they would exhibit such bad behavior. Asking first in an almost civilized way. That got them into my presence. But once they accomplished that, they took my master keys without even asking, and entered your villa. Overcome by a gang of Irish hoodlums. Hoodlums in uniform! That's who they allow to enlist in the army these days, imagine!"

"No warrant, no due process," she ranted on. "I know our rights as Americans. But do you think that traitor to his class in Washington respects our rights? They left with boxes of utensils and glassware—peculiar thieves. They even left a receipt, imagine! Most disruptive. But worry not, our housekeeping staff will put all to rights, and I'll have our local sheriff's office notified of this breach."

"That will not be necessary, Madame. I will be vacating the premises. You may forward my trunk to a Toronto, Canada address."

"Toronto? I thought you were stationed at the Mexican embassy?"

"I will travel on in my mission, pursuing peace from a perhaps more welcoming country in the Americas. I thank you for your kind hospitality."

"But—"

"Please see that I am not disturbed. I must lie down before my journey."

"Of course, of course," she said. "Oh, Professor Boerman, I am so heartily sorry."

Toby Wheeler opened the door and ushered her out.

Adler thought quickly. First: assess the changing situation. "So. They have their proof of anthrax from my kitchen laboratory. Pack all the remaining food and my hiking gear into the truck, Tobias. The rest of my survival supplies are in the cave. It is time for me to disappear."

"We're going to Canada?"

"No, no, my dear fellow. You alone will perform that part of the ruse. I will give you a name and address in Canada, where you will wait for further instructions. The Americans will give chase in that direction, while I finish my business here, then slip across the southern border."

"What business?"

Adler did not like the look in Wheeler's eye. "Why, our pursuit of peace, of course."

"I'm not going to be your decoy. I am not leaving, *Herr Docktor*. You were my way back here. Back to Hania."

"Who has rejected your advances, no?"

"So far. But she accepted the necklace. And you've kept me on a leash so tight with our wanderings up to those caves and supplying our hideout, I haven't had time to court my Hania proper."

"We are at war. Surely, she understands your duties."

"She understands that I stole her pot. That I filled it with scorpions to hurt her friends."

"What is this?"

"It's what you told me to do! Set Navajo against Hopi."

Adler shook his head. "And we have done so to great effect. Our superiors will be pleased. But your part was accomplished in such a clumsy, traceable manner, Tobias. Now I am surprised it took them this long to locate us. My mistake. I should not have left the details up to you. No matter. Our current plan—"

"I am not going to Canada!"

Too loud. Stay calm. Adler smiled. "That, of course, is your choice, my dear fellow. I have alternative plans in place. Your road ends here."

He was sorry for what he was about to do. He was growing fond of their talks.

Tobias Wheeler was not the half-wit Alder had first thought him to be. And their conversations were certainly more stimulating than the ones he'd had with the vapid widow.

But he had already attached the noise suppressor to his Luger P-08, ready for this possibility.

Then, a quiet knock at the door. "Housekeeping."

Chapter 19

Decisions

The woman became his Hania then; her face appeared frightened like the day they lost her youngest at the county fair.

"Close your eyes," Toby counseled, pressing her hand against the wound. "Lie still."

Her eyes said she understood, before the lids descended.

He looked up. "She's dead," he told Adler.

"Is she? It seems you've failed another woman, Tobias."

Adler was lifting the rucksack to his shoulder. The murderous German would not check, not if he fell in a way that further protected her, Toby thought as he saw the flash of fire erupt again.

He heard Hania's children's laughter then, as they rode the wonder wheel together, in better days.

***

Luke watched his hands. His fingers were steady as they laced up his moccasins.

"Listen to me, Bunkie," Isaiah Morgenstern said quietly.

"I am listening."

"Spenser wants Adler taken alive."

Luke's single-minded preparations stopped. "He killed his partner, Isaiah. And shot a defenseless cleaning woman."

"Whose pile of towels and an off aim saved her life. And she helped us piece together where he has gone. And. Luke, he left a note."

"Saying—?"

"Indicating he might be willing to share valuable intelligence. But only if we send you and Kitty into his camp. Alone."

"So. He is waiting for us up there, in the canyons. Where he has all the advantages."

"I know. But they think they can turn him."

"Turn him?"

"Yes. Convince him to work for us. Feed us information, feed them disinformation. Become a double agent."

"Who thinks this, Isaiah?"

"Spenser's superiors. They think Adler's knowledge of the Abwehr and where their spies are operating in the Americas would be worth the risk."

"Our risk. Our sacrifice. Kitty's and mine."

"Bunkie, if I were you, I'd finish the guy, once and for all. Then come down, and spit in the eye of them that gave you that order."

The horses approached them like a school of fish. Soon, they formed tight circles with each other, with pairs sharing mutual scratches. Luke moved closer. His hand grazed Kitty's back.

"You're one of them," she observed.

He leaned over, his nose strafing her shoulder, the side of her neck. "We both are, I think. The horses trust us. They believe all is safe. It is up to us to keep it so for them."

"Luke, how can we do this?"

He scanned the horizon, much as the sentry horse of the herd was doing. Then he scanned her the same way, from head to toe.

"Did my grandmother wrap your legs to the knee?"

"Yes."

"Good. She knows best. Learned how on the Long Walk to Bosque Redondo. They will protect you from thorns and snake bites."

He went back to his horizon sentry duty. "I did not like saying goodbye to that first class of Marines," he said quietly. "But I was proud of them. They are Diné warriors. They will use our language, their radio skills to fight for country. Not for government that has impoverished their families during Collier's misguided attempts at bettering our communities in the 1930s. These men looked past wrongs. They will protect our homeland, their sacred part of Mother Earth. I wished to go with them. Instead, this."

"Which we will accomplish together."

"I do not see a way forward. Adler is lying. He said those things to have his best chance to kill us."

"We know that, my darling. He does not. That is our weapon."

Anaba Bowman came forward. The horses nodded, greeting her. She pressed her Scottish clan blanket into Kitty's arms. "It is colder up there, once the sun goes down," she said. "Bear Man's blanket will provide."

They made their way up to the canyon of the cutout caves as far as they could with their horses, then left them in the shade of a pinon tree. Untethered. Luke knew they would come when called back.

Then, on foot, their hunt began.

Chapter 20

Duel

Americans were indecisive, Adler thought. Waiting, always waiting to enter into wars. Endlessly discussing, arguing. It had played to Hitler's advantage, of course, letting all factions of the Isolationist bikers, making it harder for Roosevelt to render aid to Britain. But how would any good German have guessed that these undisciplined people would stop going to singing, dancing movies and send even their women to work on their war machine?

Were they doing it now? Down below him? Were they discussing his value, whether he was worth enlisting as their spy? It was what his own superiors had already done, of course, downgrading him to observing internment camps at a distance, and drinking cocktails with a silly travelogue writer on the side of Mexican volcanoes.

His two targets would not want any part of enlisting him. They would come for the kill, the same as he. He wished he had known they were right under his nose sooner. That damned filmmaker had made him soft, reclusive, dependent on Wheeler for information, for operation. Had he known, he would have gone after Luke Kayenta's family, eliminated them all, along with the family Wheeler was moonstruck over. What had the Americans' own Colonel Chivington said before slaughtering Cheyenne women and children? Oh yes. "Nits make lice."

Still, Adler did not think it would take until after dark. He had never spent a night in this place. It was growing cold. His own fault. More of his going soft. It mattered not. He had supplies enough to last days, not hours. He would need to rest. Best set some traps, and he hoped, when Kayenta and his woman encountered one, it would leave enough of them to talk to before he finished them off.

The sounds started, deep in the night. Animals. Sifting winged bats, unearthly screeches of panthers. He built his fire up higher. None of the canyon's animals would dare come near him, would they? Where was the panther that Wheeler was always talking about? Then, a rustle in his woodpile. And laughter, echoing off the walls. A child's laughter. A child lived here, in this abandoned city? Yes, there he was! His head tied in rags. A tattered blue military school uniform. Stealing his wood, skittering past. Where was he going? Laughing. Mischievous. Was he also unsetting the traps Adler had set against his enemies? He reached for his pistol. There he was! Near the first trap. Adler fired, missed. Then the second. What cowards these Americans were! Sending an Indian child to sabotage his traps. A brave, laughing boy.

He fired twice more.

Still laughing, this lucky, lucky boy. Was his aim that far off?

Where had the boy gone? Back to his fire, to warm himself, and steal more wood? The audacity. He'd grab him.

There!

But he missed, took hold of a log from his stocked pile instead.

Until the log came alive in his hand. And he saw its fangs.

***

Once they heard the gunshots, Kitty stepped up the pace behind him, shining her flashlight on his future footfalls.

"Oh, Luke, be careful! Watch for—"

But she ran into his back, as he was suddenly stock still.

His gun was drawn, but the other arm folded around her as she heard the shot. The snake's opened mouth bounced off the buckskin ties of her moccasins before it skittered down the rockface.

She heard Luke's quiet voice. It was not speaking to her. "Diamondback. Viper, venomous, Herr Adler. You will be dead within hours if we do not get you help."

"But I require only one of you for assistance, Corporal, as your boy has run off again."

"Boy?"

"The laughing scoundrel that my bullets are not fast enough to reach. But you are well within my sightline, Corporal, Mrs. Charante. Who would like to usher me into the service of your government? Or, better yet, shall I kill you both, then whistle for your boy to deliver me into the arms of your secret service?"

Kitty felt a wave of panic. She tried to see around Luke. "Nastas!" she called the name of Luke's most adventurous nephew. "Stay hidden!"

Luke's strong arm was enough to keep her safe. She felt the bullet's velocity as it whizzed by her ear. He glanced back, then his arm relaxed. "Last one," he said to their enemy.

He advanced.

Adler fired, then fired again. To no effect but clicks from his gun's emptied chambers.

Luke reached Helmut Adler before his damaged hand made it to the knife strapped to his khaki trousers' leg. Kitty removed it as Luke held the man down.

The blade caught a reflection of her own eyes in the campfire's light.

"Do not let this chance go by, Mrs. Charante," Adler dared her to do what those eyes she hardly recognized as her own wanted to do.

"Not our orders," Luke said quietly, restoring her balance.

She looked up at the alcove's ceiling, blackened by centuries of woodsmoke. "Nastas!" she again called Luke's nephew out of hiding.

"Miss Kitty! He is below. With me," a female voice, Sophie Denet's voice, answered. She stood a few steps down, holding the reins of one of her sure-footed mules. She threw a rope up to Luke. "Truss that fellow up, Corporal. My Sally will get him down without any more nonsense out of him."

Kitty looked around, confused. "But, Nastas…"

"He is below, love," Luke assured her. "Safe. We are finished here." He looked deep into the cave's chambers. "Ahéheé," he whispered, thanking someone she could not see.

Chapter 21

The Woman's Dance

It was an unprecedented gathering. Suddenly, at dawn, the usually deserted crossroads was filled with people—traveling by horse, mule, donkey, car, truck, or army jeep. Some were dressed in full regalia or dress uniforms, others in workday clothing or army fatigues. They gathered around a beat-up ladder with a carefully lettered sign attached. Kitty smiled. The dress code was clearly: come as you wish to this event.

At the top of the sign was a symbol used for centuries—the whirlwind, the whirling log, in simple form. Slashed through it was an X made from strips of white birch bark.

Besides their guests, four representatives of four nations, the Papago desert people, the Apache, the Hopi, and the Navajo, stood. One by one, they approached, took up a pen and signed below the proclamation, which read:

> *Because the above ornament, which*
> *has been a symbol of friendship*
> *among our forefathers for many*
> *centuries,*

*has been desecrated recently
by other nations of peoples,
therefore, it is resolved that,
henceforth, from this date
and on forevermore,
our tribes renounce the use of the
emblem commonly known as
the swastika
on our blankets, baskets, art objects,
sandpainting, and clothing.*

A man in a pin-striped suit captured a photograph as Luke's shy sister Taswan signed her name.

Below the proclamation was a beautiful basket with the simple design woven into it with red dye. It was not made for use. Once the proclamation was signed by all who wished to, it was lit aflame.

As it burned, service people saluted the people of the four tribes and their resolution.

And then, they all went on with their day, whether herding sheep, farming crops and orchards, working to maintain the railroad, telegraph, or telephone lines, or training to fight the forces of fascism.

That night's gathering was more intimate. It belonged only to the invited group of the Navajo people. This part of Luke's Enemyway ceremony was supposed to have occurred after sundown on the first day. Well, the timing was right, if the day was delayed, Kitty thought, as she looked out the window of Taswan's hogan. The sun and sky had conspired to paint the horizon in dazzling deep reds, oranges, lavenders, and greys. Kitty felt like a girl again, being fussed over by her sister Anya before her first dance at the Armory. But it was Luke's women fussing over her now. They had dressed her to match them, in long three-tiered calico skirts, and a purple cotton velveteen blouse clinched by a wide woven red sash belt. Grandmother Anaba then started at her feet, wrapping buckskin moccasins around her ankles, folding and tying until they were midway up her calf. "We dress as the corn grows," she explained, "from the earth to the sun." Then Luke's sisters provided the loan of bracelets and rings that had been in their family for generations, decorating her right side, then her left, finally placing her own necklace of silver and turquoise squash blossoms at her throat, a gift from Luke, who had hammered out the silver. Finally, Bly Kayenta worked her shorter hair into a semblance of a *tsiiyééł* bun tie.

"You may dance all night," Tasman informed her. "And accept dance fees from any who is not in your clan or close family."

"That would be all the men," Chooli said with a laugh.

Kitty snorted. "I don't expect to get rich. Bruise too many toes and word will be out that I'm no bargain."

"Oh, no," Chooli assured her. "You were a good student of our two-step and skip steps. The Girl's Dance is not as complex as your Peabody or Jitterbug. You'll see."

"Just pace yourself," Taswan counseled.

Luke's grandmother touched her cheek. "The chindi of all your slain will be banished," Anaba Bowman declared quietly. Kitty thought of her slashing at Helmut Adler's arm underwater, of his taunting eyes as Luke held him down on the rock. Anaba nodded. "That is why he ran from his Enemyway, I think maybe," she said. "He wanted you included in this protection, Yanaha."

They would need it, Kitty thought, for the battles ahead. As Adler disappeared into the workings of the Office of Strategic Services networks in the war against the Nazis, Luke would now be stationed Westward with the next class of Code Talkers, to fight the deadly might of their ally, Japan. She was not ready for their parting, but never would be. She only hoped Jack Spenser would pull the strings necessary for her to be working close by. They were already planning to spend their furlough together in Hawaii before further orders. She would not think past her preparations for that, for now.

She had one more question for Luke's grandmother. "Mrs. Bowman, the day I arrived here, why did you give me the plaid blanket?"

"For safekeeping. To help you remember that this is one of your heart places. Bear

Man's blanket lives in our family's past. In our story. You are another story. Of being lost and found by us, like him. So, the blanket has been waiting for you, maybe. I have dreamed this."

"It is hard for me to think of a future," Kitty admitted one of her deepest secrets to those kind eyes.

"I know," Anaba Bowman said quietly. "The blanket will remind you." A small, girlish giggle burst from her lips. "So will my grandson, when you lie together on it."

When Kitty walked outside with the women and saw Luke, her breath caught in her throat. Gone was his Marine uniform or any hybrid version of it he wore when they worked together. The man before her, mounted on his brown pinto, Yuma, who seemed to be dancing already, looked exactly what he was, Navajo to his core, despite his short hair under his wide-brimmed hat. His shirt was a simplified version of the women's in deep blue velveteen, with its silverwork conch belt slung low. The denim pants were decorated with silver, too, their legs split like a Mexican gaucho's, so that his high-laced fancy beaded moccasins were on almost full display.

He slipped off Yuma and walked straight to a group of young men. She knew this part of the dance, but it still shocked her, standing there among the women and giggling children. He was ignoring her.

The drumming began.

Kitty walked over to the group of men and linked her right arm with Luke's. She turned to them. Chanting added to the beating drums and rattles. Luke looked nervous, like a bridegroom, Kitty thought as he glanced down at the necklace he'd made for her.

They danced back and forth, up and down, moving to the staccato beat. When she went forward, he went back. When she went back, he moved forward. Always, she must be in control, his women had schooled her. He knew. He understood. She led him clockwise, to acknowledge his pain, the loss of his clan brother, his injuries. She led him counterclockwise into healing and restoration. He followed her movements relentlessly.

When the chanting ended, they stopped for a long moment. Utterly still. Then she put out her hand, expectant.

Luke dug into his pocket, produced a coin, and pressed it into her palm. Kitty looked down. It was a gold piece.

"1933 St. Gaudens Double Eagle. Twenty dollars," he whispered, his forehead touching hers.

"Luke. I've never even seen one of these."

He shrugged. "I needed the right coin. Mr. Spenser said it is used in international trading. I admired it because I thought the image of Lady Liberty looked like you. It was not a gift. I traded him a good turquoise-studded silver wrist cuff for it."

"But your sisters said the dances cost five cents to a quarter."

He smiled, casting quick, murderous glances at the patiently waiting young Diné men around them. "Was it enough?" he asked. "Have I bought our first dance?"

"First, last, and all those in between," she promised.

The End

Glossary

Saiah naaghai bikieh hózhó......Navajo philosophy in a nutshell, translated

as the greeting "Walk in Beauty"

Bilagáana..........................White person (Navajo)

Tiposi.................................baby (Hopi)

Mani.................................Leader (Hopi)

Tsiiyéél............................traditional hair bun (Navajo)

Adits'ah............................Luke Kayenta's Navajo name (He Understands)

Yanaha..............................Kitty Charante's Navajo name (She Meets the Enemy)

Yei.................benevolent spirit mediators between humans and the Great Spirit

Chindi.............................a negative spirit left by a deceased person

Aoo....................................yes, we are in agreement

Ingu....................................my mother (Hopi)

Um Waynuma?...................greeting, formal (Hopi)

Ahéé.....................................greeting, informal (Hopi)

From the World War II Navajo Code

Ne he mah.........America, Our Mother
Jay sho ....buzzard, bomber plane
A ye shi................eggs, bombs
Lo tso...................whale, battleship
Besh-lo..................iron fish, submarine

Author's Notes

The seeds of the Navajo Code Talker series were planted on a trip my family and I took to Arizona many years ago, when our children were young. We had stopped on a cliffside overlooking the Painted Desert. My husband, children, and I experienced the magnificent summer sunset in the company of a Navajo man and his young son. Our daughter Marya began a colored charcoal drawing so that we would remember the splendid, changing display as the sun's light descended. In the profound silence we shared, I thought that if I ever wrote a story featuring Navajo people, I would like it to honor this moment when we blended our two families over a sacred time. I went back a generation, to my parents' time during World War II, to do it in The Navajo Code Talker Chronicles.

The Code Talkers*

Native American Code Talkers served during both World Wars I and II. There were two types of coded messages. Type 1 involved special coded/encoded vocabularies between the Native American and English languages. Type 2 was the direct use of Native American words.

200

At least 17 different Nations used their native language during World War II in every major campaign in the Pacific and Europe.

In 1989, the French Government honored the Comanche Code Talkers by presenting them with the *Chevalier of the National Order of Merit*, the highest honor France can bestow.

On November 20, 2013, the U.S. government officially honored and bestowed Congressional Native American Code Talkers Gold Medals to over 30 Indian nations in Washington, D.C.

Code Talkers of World War I

Cherokee - Type 2
Choctaw – Type 1
Osage – Type 2
Cheyenne – Type 2
Comanche – Type 2
Yankton Sioux – Type 2

Code Talkers of World War II

Assiniboine – Type 2
Cherokee – Type 2
Choctaw – Type 2
Crow – Type 2
Kaw (Kansa) – Type 2
Menominee – Type 2

Muscogee/Creek – Type 2
Navajo – Type 1
Sioux – Type 2
Canadian Cree – Type 2
Chippewa/Oneida – Type 2
Comanche – Type 1
Hopi – Type 1
Kiowa – Type 2
Meskwaki (Sac and Fox) – Type 1
Seminole – Type 2
Pawnee – Type 2

*Information prepared by the Arizona Commission of Indian Affairs – February 2007 and Hopi Veterans Services, March 2015

Indian Code Talkers served in all three continents where World War II raged. Navajo (Marines) and Hopi (Army) were in the Pacific, Comanches fought Germans in Europe, and Meskwakis' codes helped defeat them in North Africa.

The Navajo Code was never broken. Based on their unwritten language, the system allowed the Code Talkers to translate three lines of English in 20 seconds. Sending clear, error-free messages was crucial in the efforts of the Marine Corps in the Pacific Theater of World War II.
The Navajo Code Talkers kept the secret of their part in winning the war for the Allies

for a generation. Why? The code was so successful, the U.S. government thought it might be used in subsequent conflicts. Only when they were granted permission, in 1968, did the code talkers begin to divulge their efforts. And so, they honored two secrets on behalf of their country, a country that only granted them the right to vote as American citizens in 1924.

The last of the first class of Code Talkers has now died. Only one who served, Chester Nez, ever wrote an autobiography. Their stories have become history. History is where historical fiction lives.

Family Connections

With my mother's death at age 102 years in 2021, my parents' long and beautiful lives have now passed into history, too. Like Kitty's fictional family, they grew up on the West Side of New York City, as new Americans, the children of immigrants from Ireland, Croatia, and French Canada. My father and my mother's brothers served in World War II. My mom traveled to my father's stateside postings in the South and Seattle, before he was sent overseas. I've borrowed parts of their lives to tell my story.

Captain or Corporal?

Luke is referred to as Captain or Corporal in *All of Me*. Those who know his rank in the Office of Strategic Service (O.S.S., the wartime precursor of the Central

Intelligence Agency, or C.I.A.) use the one he'd achieved in that branch of the service—captain. The O.S.S. used standard U.S. military ranks for its officers and enlisted personnel, but it maintained a notably informal and non-military culture compared to the conventional armed forces.

In the Marines, Luke was a corporal. Both are leaders who have authority over soldiers.

The Navajo Code Talkers were not assigned specific military ranks. None were higher-ranking commissioned officers. Many earned individual medals for their service. Their unique skill was later recognized with official commendations from the highest levels of the military and Congress. After decades of obscurity, the Navajo Code Talkers Recognition Act of 2000 authorized the presentation of Congressional Gold Medals to the Navajo and other Native American Code Talker veterans.

Luke's Hair
The Navajo Code Talkers were Marines and so complied with the service's strict dress and grooming rules. So, in the Navajo Code Talker series, Luke wears his hair short.

In 2024, a Native American service member became the first Marine in the Corps to receive a religious waiver allowing him to grow his hair long in accordance with his Navajo heritage. The authorization was a critical milestone in a long push for service members to be allowed to observe religious practices while in uniform.

This Marine's father served in the Air Force for more than twenty years. His great-grandfather served in World War II. Part of the reason for his request was to honor generations of his ancestors who served but were unable to observe their heritage while doing so.

Mildred Hemmons Carter (1921-2011)
I have used real persons fictitiously in *All of Me*. Mildred Hemmons Carter comes to the rescue with her life-saving vaccine shipment in her Piper J-3 Cub airplane. Mrs. Carter is now a Designated Original Tuskegee Airman and the first Black female pilot in Alabama. Because of her sex, she was denied admission into the Tuskegee Airmen, and because of her race, to the Women Airforce Service Pilots (W.A.S.P.). But she graduated with Tuskegee's first class of the Civilian Pilot Training Program, where she met Eleanor Roosevelt, a great admirer of the program. Mrs. Carter worked at Morton Field as Chief Clerk of the Quartermaster Corps, rigged parachutes, and operated a bulldozer to clear airstrips. I loved giving her a high-flying spy mission in my story.

William Canfield Marshall (1882-1948)
I had fun giving a cameo role in my novel to William Marshall, who once worked as a dining car waiter for the railroad. His wife Norma Arica was a kindergarten teacher who sold her wedding ring so that their son could go to law school. Their son? **Thurgood Marshall** (1908-1993), who had a great passion for Civil Rights. In 1967, he became the first African-American to serve as a Justice on the U.S. Supreme Court.

Sophie Yazzi (1914-2019),
Named Awéé Yázhi at birth, Sophie Yazzi wanted to be a Code Talker. She tried enlisting, but was denied. Johnny Manuelito, one of the original class of 29 Code Talkers, told her the Marines were not allowing women. He advised her to try the WAAC, the women's branch of the army. She did, served honorably as Tech 4 Sergeant, cooking for young aviation cadet pilots at Foster Air Force Base in Victoria, Texas. She married soon after the war, raised children and grandchildren, and tended her sheep and crops in the shadow of Canyon de Chelly, which she called "the best place on the rez."

Hundreds came to Sergeant Yazzi's funeral, including a group of National Guard in their dress blues who flew in by helicopter to honor the woman who had fed their long-ago comrades.

Other historical people mentioned or featured in *All of Me*

Carl Nelson Gorman (1907-1998) One of the original class of 29 Navajo Code Talkers, He lied about his age to enlist for the "special duty" of becoming a Code Talker...he was older than the age limit of 30. He became a successful artist. His son, R.C. Gorman (1931-2005), was even more renowned and is called "the Picasso of Native American Artists."

Staff Sergeant Philip Johnson (1892-1978) was the son of a missionary peacemaker, who grew up among the Navajo people, and really did meet President Theodore Roosevelt as a child when serving as a translator. An army engineer at the time of the war, he proposed recruiting Navajo men fluent in both their native language and English to come up with the Navajo Code. He served as a recruiter and school administrator to the highly confidential program.

Dr. Colin Ross
Code Talkers were so successful in World War I that the Germans saw them as a serious threat to their future war efforts. In the 1930s, Germany sent spies and agitators to sabotage future Code Talkers and limit the enlistment of Native Americans. German agents traveled to native nations looking to

learn about their languages. Propagandists, such as German anthropologist Dr. Colin Ross, argued that Native peoples should not sign up for the draft. He visited Native American reservations to gather information for use in the German propaganda ministry. Ross wrote articles and books, encouraging Native Americans to rebel against the government. American groups with German sympathies, such as the Silver Shirts and German American Bund, also attempted to gain Native supporters. The German American Bund financed campaigns to incite Natives in Montana and the Dakotas against the draft in 1939 and 1940.

Germany's actions against Native enlistment eventually failed. Pro-German propaganda ignored the progress America had made in rectifying some Native issues, such as poverty and autonomy. Instead, Native communities joined in droves to fight in World War II. As the Allies were closing in at the end of the war, Colin Ross and his wife committed suicide.

Karl May (1842-1912) was indeed Adolph Hitler's favorite writer since boyhood. His tales of the American West were a sort of later German version of James Fenimore Cooper's Leatherstocking series, and an earlier *Lone Ranger*. It featured German-born pioneer Old Shatterhand and his Apache companion Winnetou. Karl May had never visited the American West, and his adventure tales were highly imaginative. Hitler recommended May's books to his generals and had special editions printed for his troops on the front lines of World War II.

Big Jock McCluskey

The story Anaba Bowman tells about the Hudson's Bay Scottish trader lost in a storm is based on the life of Big Jock McCluskey, who traded machine loom blankets and shirts woven in the colors of Rob Roy tartan of the Clan MacGregor. Family stories claim that the Native Americans loved the red-black cloth and called it Buffalo Plaid. I had fun thinking of Big Jock losing his way in a Northern Arizona winter and finding the Navajo, who had been weaving their own wool for centuries! Still, one of Luke's long-ago grandmothers politely traded one of her textiles for his. It appears in *All of Me*'s story.

Medical Breakthroughs As with my citing the beginnings of penicillin research in Navajo Code Talker Chronicles Book 1, *I'll Be Seeing You*, the remedy tried on Yiska's scorpion stings by Dr. Carmichael was indeed being researched in Cincinnati. **Dr. George Rieveschl** wanted his two-part synthetic compound to improve muscle-relaxing medications. He found that it dramatically blocked histamine, a chemical released in the body that narrows air passages in the lungs and causes inflammation. This breakthrough led to Benadryl, the first antihistamine.

A Valuable Heirloom

The 1933 St. Gaudens Double Eagle twenty-dollar gold piece that Luke pays Kitty for her Woman's Dance has an interesting history, I think. It was designed in 1907 by the famous American sculptor Augustus St. Gaudens. His home is now a National Park site in New Hampshire. After its 1933 version was struck by the U.S. Mint, President Franklin Roosevelt had them recalled to be melted down to help ease the banking crisis. But a few slipped through, making them an exceedingly rare find over the years. I imagine Luke received his from O.S.S. operative Jack Spenser, as the gold piece was used in international trade. Perhaps Jack knew it would become valuable and wished to give Luke and Kitty a precious family heirloom. A 1933 St. Gaudens Double Eagle was sold at auction in 2021 for $18.9 million, making it the most expensive collector's coin ever. I hope Kitty held on to hers!

Fateful Days

The proclamation by four American Southwest Indian nations to renounce the use of the swastika in their art really happened on February 28, 1940, as a protest against Nazi acts of oppression. That was before the United States entered World War II, even earlier than I placed it in *All of Me*. Since then, some artists have called for the reclaiming of the traditional design. Others believe the generational trauma that is associated with the symbol should keep it buried forever. What do you think?

On September 11, 2001, I was on jury duty at the Federal Building in lower Manhattan. I climbed up out of the subway station that was one station away from the one that belonged to the World Trade Center. I looked up into the beautiful, cloudless sky of that day at the moment the plane hit the first tower. My city of dreams soon became a nightmare. I wrote Book 2: **Watch Over Me** as an effort to restore the beauty of the beloved island in the center of the world that held out such promise for generations of my family. I hope readers might see it as a love song to our wounded, resilient city of dreams, and the series as a love song to my parents.

Eileen Charbonneau books also published by BWL Publishing Inc.

Eileen Charbonneau is a Laramie and Heart of the West award-winning author of novels and screenplays. She's been involved with theater and independent filmmaking projects, and is a storyteller of Irish and Native American tales. Eileen's multi-cultural heritage includes grandmothers of the Ojibwe Nation and Shoshone relatives, who were three members of the Lewis and Clark Expedition.

Eileen Charbonneau's stories explore the perspectives of people often left out of history: women, first peoples, immigrants, and marginalized poor.

Eileen has published fiction for adult as well for young readers. She lives in the brave little state of Vermont with her husband Ed. Eileen loves keeping up with the lives of three interesting children and a grandchild, reading, watching great movies, exploring her beautiful state, country and world, roots music and dance of all cultures, and Vermont maple creemies. (write to her at eileencharbonneau@gmail.com, and she'll tell you what _they_ are!)

Eileen loves to hear from readers. You
can find her at:
https://bookswelove.net/charbonneau-
eileen/
email: eileencharbonneau@gmail.com
twitter: @EileenC1988
Facebook: Eileen Charbonneau Author
Instagram: eileencharbonneau

Blogs: http://manituwak.blogspot.com
https://bwlauthors.blogspot.com